The Testament

JOHN GRISHAM

Level 6

Retold by Karen Holmes
Series Editors: Andy Hopkins and Jocelyn Potter

Pearson Education Limited
Edinburgh Gate, Harlow,
Essex CM20 2JE, England
and Associated Companies throughout the world.

ISBN: 978-1-4058-8274-3

First published in the UK by Century 1999
First published by Penguin Books Ltd 2001
This edition published 2008

3 5 7 9 10 8 6 4 2

Typeset by Graphicraft Ltd, Hong Kong
Set in 11/14pt Bembo
Printed in China
SWTC/02

Published by Pearson Education Ltd in association with
Penguin Books Ltd, both companies being subsidiaries of Pearson Plc

For a complete list of the titles available in the Penguin Readers series please write to your local
Pearson Longman office or to: Penguin Readers Marketing Department, Pearson Education,
Edinburgh Gate, Harlow, Essex CM20 2JE, England.

Contents

		page
Introduction		v
Chapter 1	The Last Day	1
Chapter 2	Troy Phelan's Testament	5
Chapter 3	Nate's Mission	12
Chapter 4	Into the Pantanal	19
Chapter 5	The Slide	23
Chapter 6	Legal Challenges	28
Chapter 7	Alligators and Indians	34
Chapter 8	The Missionary	44
Chapter 9	A Death	52
Chapter 10	Fever	60
Chapter 11	A New Beginning	68
Chapter 12	A Letter to Rachel	74
Chapter 13	The Lawsuit	80
Chapter 14	The Settlement	87
Chapter 15	Return to the Pantanal	93
Activities		100

Introduction

"Stop!" someone shouts, and they're moving behind me. I grab the handle and open the door. The air is very cold. I step onto the narrow balcony and, without looking down, I throw myself over the edge.

Troy Phelan is one of the richest men in the United States. He is eccentric, hates his three ex-wives and his six children, and is ready to die. He takes his own life on December 9, 1996—just before Christmas and New Year's, that special time for family celebrations.

After his death, his family gathers to collect his money. But Phelan has played one last, cruel trick on them; he has left his fortune to an unknown illegitimate daughter—and nobody knows exactly where she is.

Nate O'Riley is a powerful Washington lawyer who has lived too hard for too long. He is in the hospital, recovering from his addiction to alcohol and drugs. Returning to the outside world will be difficult but he has to do it. He knows there will be temptations. Can he resist? Can he do the job his firm is giving him? Will he be able to find Rachel Lane, Phelan's illegitimate daughter, who is a missionary somewhere on the Brazil-Bolivia border? And if he does find her, will she accept her father's money?

Nate sets out to find Rachel in the Pantanal, a 140,000 square kilometer area of swamp, on Christmas Eve, 1996. He knows he is not going to get a warm welcome if he does find her. She will probably not appreciate being found and the Indians she is living among prefer no contact with outsiders. And there are plenty of hungry alligators who would like to see him fall over the side of the boat. But, Nate's journey from the tense courtrooms of Washington to the wild jungles of Brazil teaches him about another, better way of life.

The Testament is a story of the battle between good and evil, and between charity and self-interest.

John Grisham, the author of this book, was born on 8 February 1955 in Jonesboro, Arkansas. His father was a building worker and the family was poor. They moved frequently until 1967 when they settled in Southaven, Mississippi. Grisham's mother encouraged him to read when he was young, and his love of books began. He graduated in 1977 from Mississippi State University and went from there to the University of Mississippi to study law, graduating in 1981. At first, he studied tax law but then changed to criminal law. After graduating, Grisham started his own law firm in Southaven. In 1983, he was elected to the Mississippi House of Representatives, where he served until 1990. While working in politics, he continued his law practice.

In 1984, he started writing while working full-time. He got up at 5 AM each day so he could spend a few hours writing before going to the office. His first book, *A Time to Kill* (1989), did not sell well, but success soon followed. *The Firm* (1991) was a number one best-seller, and the movie rights were sold for $600,000. Grisham gave up his law practice immediately and concentrated on writing. He has written one novel a year since then; many are best-sellers, and he was named the best-selling novelist of the 1990s.

Novels by Grisham in the Penguin Readers and Penguin Active Reading series are: *A Time to Kill, The Firm, The Pelican Brief, The Client, The Rainmaker, The Runaway Jury, The Partner, The Street Lawyer,* and *The Brethren*.

More recent Grisham novels include *The Innocent Man* (2006), about a man who is wrongfully sent to prison in Oklahoma, and *Playing for Pizza* (2007), a comic novel about American football played in Italy.

Grisham and his wife Renee have two children. They own a large farm in Mississippi and another near Charlottesville, Virginia.

Grisham has a special interest in the Pantanal region of Brazil. The Pantanal is the world's largest freshwater wetland. The variety of wildlife makes it one of the world's greatest natural wonders. Grisham and a friend, a missionary in Brazil, went there together before Grisham wrote this novel. In Grisham's words, "we had a wonderful time for four days counting alligators, photographing wildlife . . . eating black beans and rice, telling stories, all from a boat that somehow grew smaller."

In *The Testament*, Grisham takes his readers to the Pantanal to learn about the native people—and about their suffering at the hands of Europeans. After the Portuguese explorer Pedro Alvarcs Cabral discovered Brazil in 1500, more and more Europeans, especially from Portugal and Spain, settled there. The native Indians fought the Europeans, but their weapons were less effective. Europeans brought with them another kind of weapon—disease. The Indian population fell from about five million in 1500 to 270,000 in 1999. In fact, their enemies included an agency of their own government, who in the period up to 1967 attempted to destroy them completely.

In Chapter 7, Nate's guide asks him if he has ever heard of Hidrovia and explains that it is a project to link Brazil, Bolivia, Paraguay, Argentina, and Uruguay by creating a shipping channel. The original plan was developed in 1997. The future for it is still uncertain. There has been a lot of opposition to this project because it would greatly reduce the size of the wetlands. There are new studies investigating it, but according to the International Rivers Network these studies suggest even greater removal of rock between Corumbá and the Apa River in the Pantanal.

Chapter 1   The Last Day

It's the last day, even the last hour now. I'm an old man, lonely and unloved, sick and hurting, and tired of living. I am ready for death; it has to be better than this.

I own this tall glass building, the land around it, and the 2,000 people who work here. I own silver in Nevada, coffee in Kenya, and coal in Angola. My company owns businesses that produce electricity, make computers, and print books. I'm worth more than eleven billion dollars.

The money is my greatest problem.

I had three families—three ex-wives, who had seven children. They're gathering here today because I'm dying and it's time to divide the money. I don't care who gets the money. But I do care very much who doesn't get it.

My first wife was Lillian. We married young—I was twenty-four and she was eighteen—and had four children. Her oldest boy is now forty-seven. Troy Junior, or T.J., was thrown out of college when he was nineteen for selling drugs. I gave him, like the others, five million dollars on his twenty-first birthday. It ran like water through his fingers.

T.J.'s brother, Rex, is forty-four. Our oldest daughter is Libbigail, a child I loved desperately until she went to college and forgot about me. She married an African and I took her name out of my will. Our younger daughter, Mary Ross, is married to a doctor. He wants to be super-rich but they're heavily in debt.

All Lillian's children are the same. They're in debt and unemployable, and they want my money.

After Lillian, I married my secretary, Janie, a beautiful young thing, twenty-two years younger than me. She had two children.

1

The younger one, Rocky, was killed in a car with two of his friends. Her daughter Geena is married to a fool who could lose half a billion dollars in three years.

I married Tira when I was sixty-four. She was twenty-three and pregnant with Ramble. He's now fourteen and has already been arrested once for theft and once for possession of drugs. He has rings in his ears, eyebrows, and nose. Like the others, he expects to get rich, to get a fortune because I'm his father.

I know these people. I watch them.

♦

Snead appears from another room. He's been my servant for almost thirty years now.

"How are you sir?" he asks.

I say nothing because I'm neither required nor expected to respond to Snead.

"Some coffee, sir?"

"Lunch."

Snead expects to get rich too. He wants me to die because he expects a few million. The trouble with having money is that everybody wants a little of it. Snead's name is not mentioned in my will.

He brings in my lunch. The final meal.

Later, Snead pushes my wheelchair out of the apartment, down the hall, through another door. The room is full of lawyers and psychiatrists who will decide whether I'm sane. There are cameras pointing at me. Every whisper, every move, every breath will be recorded. I'm sitting here to prove to the world that I am sane enough to make a new will.

Each family has hired a psychiatrist. Their names are printed on cards in front of them—Dr. Zadel, Dr. Flowe, Dr. Theishen. I study their eyes and faces. They expect me to be crazy, but I'm going to prove them wrong.

Josh Stafford is speaking. "My name is Josh Stafford and I am the lawyer for Mr. Troy Phelan. The psychiatrists in this room will examine Mr. Phelan. If they believe that he is wholly sane, then he intends to sign a new will."

Stafford taps his pencil on the thick will lying before us. My families haven't seen the will, so they can only guess what it contains. They believe that the money will be divided fairly among the children, with generous gifts to my ex-wives. Stafford prepared the will and, with my permission, this is what he has implied.

The psychiatrists begin their examination. Zadel goes first. "Mr. Phelan, can you tell us the date, time, and place?"

I drop my chin to my chest like a fool and think about the question. "Monday, December 9, 1996. The place is my office."

"The time?"

"About two-thirty in the afternoon," I say.

"And where is your office?"

"McLean, Virginia."

They ask many more questions. Then Theishen says, "What is your current physical condition?"

"I'm sick. I have cancer. My doctors say I won't live more than three months."

I can feel their excitement. The rumor has been confirmed.

"Are you under the influence of drugs or alcohol?"

"No."

Back to Zadel: "Mr. Phelan, you have about eleven billion dollars. Is that correct?"

"Yes."

"Do you intend to sign a new will today?"

"Yes, I do."

"Is that the will on the table in front of you?"

"It is."

"Does that will leave a large part of your estate to your children?"

"It does."

Zadel places his pen on the table and looks at Stafford. "In my opinion, Mr. Phelan is mentally capable of signing his will."

"Do you all agree?" Stafford asks the other lawyers.

"Yes. Absolutely." They nod their heads as fast as they can.

Stafford slides the will to me and gives me a pen. I turn to the back and sign a name that nobody can read, then place my hands on top of it.

"This meeting is over," Stafford says, and everyone quickly leaves the room. One camera remains on me. I tell Snead to take a seat at the table. Stafford and one of his partners, Durban, are also seated. When we're alone, I produce an envelope from my pocket. I remove from it three pieces of yellow legal paper.

Stafford, Durban, and Snead look confused.

"This is my real will," I announce, taking a pen. "I wrote it a few hours ago. Dated today, and now signed today." I write my name again. "This replaces all previous wills, including the one I signed less than five minutes ago."

I put the papers back in the envelope and push it across the table to Stafford. At the same time, I rise from my wheelchair. My legs are shaking. Just seconds now. Surely I'll be dead before I hit the ground.

"Hey!" someone says—Snead, I think. But I'm moving away from them.

I walk, almost run, past a row of chairs to the big sliding doors, which are unlocked.

"Stop!" someone shouts, and they're moving behind me. I grab the handle and open the door. The air is very cold. I step onto the narrow balcony and, without looking down, I throw myself over the edge.

Chapter 2   Troy Phelan's Testament

Snead reached the balcony just in time to scream in horror, then he watched helplessly as Mr. Phelan fell silently, growing smaller and smaller until he struck the ground. Snead stared in disbelief, then he began to cry.

Josh Stafford was a step behind him and witnessed most of the fall. It took him a minute or two to recover from the shock and start thinking like a lawyer again. He watched the family down below collect around Phelan's body, then he went back into the room.

The camera was still on. Snead faced it, raised his right hand and swore to tell the truth, then explained what he'd just witnessed. Stafford opened the envelope and held the yellow sheets of paper close enough for the camera to see.

"Yes, I saw him sign that," Snead said. "Just seconds ago."

"Did he say this was his last will and testament?"

"He called it his testament."

Stafford made Durban repeat the same statement, then placed himself in front of the camera and gave his version of events. When he finished, he told Snead to leave the room.

Stafford turned back to the camera, and looked at the sheets of yellow paper. The first sheet was a letter. Stafford spoke to the camera: "This letter is dated today, Monday, December 9, 1996. It is addressed to me from Troy Phelan. I will read it in full.

"'Dear Josh: I am dead now. These are my instructions, and I want you to follow them closely. First, I want a quick examination of my body. Second, there will be no funeral. I want to be cremated and my ashes scattered from the air over my ranch in Wyoming. Third, I want you to keep my will secret until January 15, 1997. The law does not require you to produce it immediately. Goodbye. Troy.'"

Stafford carefully picked up the second piece of paper. "This is a one-page document. It is the last testament of Troy L. Phelan. I will read it all:

" 'The last testament of Troy L. Phelan. To each of my children, Troy Phelan Jr.,★ Rex Phelan, Libbigail Jeter, Mary Ross Jackman, Geena Strong, and Ramble Phelan, I give enough money to pay off any debts they have today. Their future debts will not be covered by this gift. If any of these children attempt to contest this will, then they will receive nothing.

" 'To my ex-wives, Lillian, Janie, and Tira, I give nothing. They were adequately provided for in the divorces.

" 'The rest of my estate I give to my daughter Rachel Lane, born on November 2, 1954, in New Orleans, Louisiana, to a woman named Evelyn Cunningham, who is now dead.' "

Stafford had never heard of these people. He paused, then went on.

" 'I appoint my trusted lawyer Josh Stafford to carry out this will. Signed, December 9, 1996, three P.M., by Troy Phelan.' "

Stafford placed it on the table and picked up the third sheet. "This is a note addressed to me again. I will read it: 'Josh: Rachel Lane is a World Tribes missionary on the Brazil–Bolivia border. She works with an Indian tribe in a region known as the Pantanal. The nearest town is Corumbá. I couldn't find her. I've had no contact with her in the last twenty years. Signed, Troy Phelan.' "

Stafford put down the last piece of paper and turned to Durban. "He thought of everything."

"He's a very cruel man," Durban said. "Can you imagine the money those fools will spend in the next month?"

"It seems a crime not to tell them."

★Jr.: the short form of Junior

6

"We can't. We have our orders."

♦

Outside Lillian's large house in Falls Church, a group of journalists waited on the street for a family member to come out. Inside, Phelan's four eldest children gathered. They tried to be serious and sad. It was difficult. Fine wine was served, lots of it. By midnight T.J. and Rex were drunk, celebrating their fabulous new wealth.

♦

The following day, Stafford met Tip Durban and together they drove to the medical examiner's office in McLean.

"The cause of death is obvious. There's no trace of alcohol or drugs," the medical examiner said. "And there was no sign of cancer. Troy was in good health at the time of his death."

"Did he tell you he had cancer?" Durban asked Stafford on the drive back.

"Yes, several times."

"Why did he lie?"

"Who knows? Everybody thought he was dying."

"Why did he jump?"

"He was a very lonely old man."

"It seems like a nasty trick," Durban said. "He promises money to his family, their psychiatrists say that he isn't crazy, then at the last minute he signs a different will. Why did he hate them so much?"

"They embarrassed him. They fought with him. They never earned an honest dime, and they spent many of his millions. Troy never planned to leave them anything."

Back at his office, Stafford talked to members of his team. "You have to find a person who, I suspect, does not want to be found."

He told them what he knew about Rachel Lane. There wasn't much. "First, find out about the World Tribes Missions. Who are they? How do they operate? How do they pick their people? Where do they send them? Everything. Find out about her mother, Evelyn Cunningham. She's dead now. Find out all you can."

♦

T.J. nursed a sore head until noon, then drank a beer. He walked around his dirty apartment. He couldn't find his wife. He and Biff had been through three fights already that day.

He opened another beer and looked at himself in the mirror in the hall. "Troy Phelan, Jr.," he said. "Son of Troy Phelan, tenth richest man in America, worth eleven billion. Yes!"

He dressed in his best suit, a gray one he'd worn yesterday when Dear Old Dad faced the psychiatrists and performed so wonderfully. "Armani, here I come," he whistled joyfully.

Life had been soft and luxurious for the first twenty years, and then he received his inheritance. His five million had disappeared before he reached thirty, and his father hated him for it.

"What can I do with half a billion dollars?" he asked himself as he drove along the highway. "Five hundred million tax-free." He began to laugh.

His first stop was the BMW-Porsche garage run by his friend, Dickie.

"Biff would like a Porsche, a red 911."

"When?"

Troy stared angrily at him. "Now."

"Sure, T.J. What about money?"

"I'll pay for it the same time I pay for my black one. Also a 911. How much are they?"

"About ninety thousand each."

"No problem. When can we have them?"

8

"In a day or two. When will you have the cash?" Dickie asked.

"In a month or two. But I want the cars now."

Dickie looked away. "Listen, T.J., I can't hand over two new cars without payment."

"Fine. I'll go somewhere else. I could buy this whole garage, you know. I could walk into any bank right now and ask for ten million or twenty million and buy this place. They would happily give me the money. Do you understand?"

Dickie's eyes narrowed. "How much did he leave you?"

"Enough to buy the bank. Are you giving me the cars or shall I go down the street?"

"Let me find the cars."

♦

Ramble spent the day in his room, smoking, listening to music, and ignoring everyone. He hadn't been to school for weeks. His lawyer had told him that the money would go into a trust until he was either eighteen or twenty-one. Until then, he would get a generous amount of money to spend every month.

He would form a band called Ramble. He would play guitar and sing and chase girls.

Two floors up Tira, his mother, spent the day on the phone chatting with friends. Most of them gossiped long enough to ask how much she might get from the estate, but she was afraid to guess. When she divorced Troy she got ten million and the house. She was now down to her last two million dollars. Her needs were so great. Her friends had beach houses in the Bahamas and she had to stay in luxury hotels. They bought their clothes in New York; she picked her clothes up locally. Their children went to the best schools, out of the way; Ramble was in the basement and wouldn't come out.

♦

Geena Phelan Strong was thirty and married to Cody, husband number two. He had big dreams, but after six months his businesses had made huge losses. The five million Troy gave Geena on her twenty-first birthday had shrunk to less than a million, and their debts were growing. Then Troy jumped from the window.

They spent the morning looking for homes in Swinks Mill, the place of their grandest dreams. By dusk they were looking at an empty house priced at four and a half million and seriously considering making an offer.

◆

Rex, age forty-four, brother of T.J., was under criminal investigation. A bank had failed and the FBI was making fierce inquiries. He owed more than seven million dollars. Now Troy was dead, Rex could stop worrying. He could pay his debts and play with his money.

He spent the day with Hark Gettys, his lawyer. He wanted the money quickly, desperately, and he pressured Gettys to call Josh Stafford.

"We have to see that will!" he shouted at Hark throughout the day. Hark calmed him with a long lunch and good wine. Amber, Rex's wife, dropped by and found them both drunk. She wasn't angry. She loved Rex more than ever now.

Hark Gettys was excited. The old man was dead, and his crazy family was a lawyer's dream. This was his chance to start his own company and to make a lot of money. He wanted a long fight over the will, a fight that would make him famous and rich.

◆

According to the internet, the World Tribes Missions' headquarters was in Houston, Texas. Their goal was to spread Christianity around the world, and they had 4,000 missionaries working with native peoples. Twenty-eight Indian tribes in Brazil were being ministered to by World Tribes missionaries. These missionaries received training in living in the jungle, languages, and medical skills.

So, Rachel lived in a hut and slept on a bed she'd built herself and cooked over a fire. She ate food she'd grown or trapped and killed, and taught Bible stories to the children and the adults. She knew nothing, and certainly cared nothing, for the worries and pressures of the world.

"We may never find her," Durban said. "No phones, no electricity. You have to climb through the mountains to get to these people."

"We have no choice," Josh said. "We called the World Tribes Missions and they won't tell us anything. They wouldn't even confirm that this woman exists. But I have an idea. We have to send someone to find Rachel Lane, right? And we can't just send anyone. It has to be a lawyer, someone who can explain what's happening. And it has to be someone from our company. But it's not going to be a quick trip. Brazil's a big country. We're talking jungles and mountains. These people have never seen a car. It might take at least a week."

"So who do we send?" Durban asked.

"What about Nate?"

Nate O'Riley was a partner who was, at the moment, locked away in a private hospital in the Blue Ridge Mountains. In the past ten years he'd been a frequent visitor to this hospital, each time trying to stop drinking and taking drugs. Now, at the age of forty-eight, he had no money, was twice divorced, and the government was chasing him for nonpayment of taxes.

"He used to be an outdoor type, didn't he?" Durban asked.

"Oh yeah. Rock climbing, diving, all that crazy stuff. Then the slide into alcoholism began and he stopped all that."

The slide had begun in his mid-thirties. He was a star in the legal practice but he began drinking heavily and using drugs. He ignored his family, and then he lost a lawsuit and fell apart. The firm sent him to a hospital to recover. He could stay clean for months, even years, but he always crashed.

Four months earlier, he'd locked himself in a hotel room with a bottle of vodka and a sack of pills. Josh sent him to the hospital for the fourth time in ten years.

"It might be good for him," Durban said. "You know, to get away for a while."

Chapter 3   Nate's Mission

Nate walked to his window and looked at the Shenandoah Valley 1,000 meters below. It was covered with new snow. He remembered that it was almost Christmas and the thought saddened him. The kids were gone now, either grown or taken away by their mothers. The last thing Nate wanted was another Christmas in a bar with other drunks.

Breakfast was black coffee, which he had with his nurse, Sergio. For the last four months, Sergio had also been his best friend. He knew everything about the miserable life of Nate O'Riley.

"You have a guest today. Mr. Stafford," Sergio said.

"Wonderful."

Josh had visited once a month. Nate was resting in his room when Josh arrived.

"You look great," Josh said. "How are you doing?"

"I need to get out of here, Josh."

"Your doctor says another week or two."

"Great. Then what? Can I come back to the company?"

"Not so fast, Nate. You have a couple of problems. We can deal with the bankruptcy but that still leaves the problem of your taxes."

From 1992 to 1995, Nate had failed to report about sixty thousand dollars in other income.

"So what am I supposed to do?" Nate asked. "Do you think I'm going to prison?"

"Troy Phelan died," Josh said, and it took Nate a second to understand.

"I didn't know. When did he die?"

"Four days ago. Jumped out of a window. He'd just signed two wills—the first prepared by me; the second, and last, he wrote himself. Then he jumped. He left everything to an illegitimate daughter I'd never heard of. I want you to find her."

"Me?"

"Yes. We don't know where she is."

"How much did he—?"

"About eleven billion, before taxes."

"Does she know it?"

"No. She doesn't even know he's dead."

"Where is she?"

"Brazil, we think. She's a missionary working with a tribe of Indians."

"How long will I be gone?" Nate asked.

"It's a wild guess, but I'd say ten days. There's no hurry and she might be hard to find."

"What part of the country?"

"West, near Bolivia. This mission she works for sends its people into the jungles, where they minister to Indians from the Stone Age."

"You want me to find the right jungle, then walk into it to find the right tribe of Indians. I tell them I'm a friendly lawyer from the States and they should help me find a woman who probably doesn't want to be found."

"Something like that. Think of it as an adventure. Someone has to go, Nate. A lawyer from our firm has to meet this woman face to face, show her a copy of the will, explain it to her, and find out what she wants to do next. It can't be done by a Brazilian lawyer."

"And if I say no?" Nate asked.

Josh smiled. "We'll find someone else. Think of it as a vacation. You're not afraid of the jungle, are you?"

"Of course not."

"Then go have some fun. You can leave next week."

"I'll be there for the holidays. That's a great idea."

"You want to miss Christmas? What about your kids?"

There were four of them, two by each wife. One in graduate school and one in college, two in middle school.

"I haven't heard from them."

"I'm sorry," Josh said. He'd certainly heard from the families. Both wives had lawyers who'd called to ask for money. Nate's oldest child needed money for college fees. He'd called Josh, not to ask about his father's health but, more important, to ask about his father's share of the firm's profits last year.

"Is it in the Amazon?"

"No, the Pantanal, the largest wetlands in the world."

"What happens when I get back? Do I have my office? Am I still a partner?"

"I don't know, Nate. This is your fourth time in the hospital in ten years. If you went back now, you'd go back to the office and be the world's greatest lawyer for six months. You'd ignore the old friends, the old bars, the old neighborhoods. You'd work, work, work. Then there'd be a crack somewhere. An old friend might find you. A girl from another life. You'll slide again. I don't want that to happen."

14

"A couple of weeks in the Brazilian wetlands is beginning to sound good," Nate said.

"So you'll go?"

"Yes."

Josh left him a thick file on the Phelan estate and its mysterious new heir. And there were two books on the Indians of South America. Nate read for eight hours. He was suddenly anxious to begin his adventure. When Sergio checked on him, he was sitting on the bed, papers around him, lost in another world.

"It's time for me to leave," Nate said.

"Yes, it is," Sergio replied.

♦

The heirs collected huge debts. They signed contracts for new houses. New cars were delivered. They hired people to find the right private jet and give advice about what horse to buy. Several lawyers were fired, and new ones were brought in to replace them.

♦

The Phelan case landed on the desk of Judge F. Parr Wycliff. He was thrilled to get such a famous lawsuit and called Josh Stafford to introduce himself.

"Is there a will?" Wycliff asked.

"Yes, there is a will."

"Where is it? When will the money be released?"

"I have it," Josh said. "My client asked me to wait until January 15."

"Why?"

The reason was simple. Troy wanted his greedy children to spend a lot of money before they found out he hadn't left them anything.

15

"I have no idea," Josh said.

"What's in the will?"

"I can't tell you."

"I'm a little sympathetic to the Phelan family," Wycliff said. "They have a right to know what's in the will. I think we should read it to them on December 27."

Josh wanted to laugh. Gather them all together, the Phelans and their lawyers and their new friends. Make sure the newspapers know about it. He could hear the crying and the cursing as the Phelans tried to understand what their father had done to them. Suddenly, Josh couldn't wait.

"The twenty-seventh's fine with me," he said.

"Good," Wycliff said. "I'll let everybody know. There are lots of lawyers."

"It helps if you remember that there are six kids and three ex-wives, so there are nine principal sets of lawyers."

"I hope my courtroom is big enough."

"I suggest *you* read the will," Josh said.

Wycliff intended to. He imagined what would happen. People crowded together, not a sound as the envelope was opened. This would be one of his finest moments, reading a will that gave away eleven billion dollars.

"I assume the will is—interesting," the Judge said.

"It's very interesting."

The Judge actually smiled.

♦

As usual, Josh had carefully planned Nate's release. He arrived at the hospital with a bag full of clothes, a passport, tickets, and plenty of cash.

"How do you feel?" Josh asked as they drove south.

"Could you stop at the nearest store?"

16

"Sure. Why?"

"I'd like to get some beer."

"Very funny."

"I'd kill for a tall Coca-Cola."

Back in the car, Josh said, "Your flight goes to São Paulo, then you'll go on to a city called Campo Grande."

"Do these people speak English?"

"No. They're Brazilian. They speak Portuguese."

"How big is Campo Grande?"

"Half a million, but it's not your destination. From there you'll catch a flight to a place called Corumbá. There you'll meet a lawyer named Valdir Ruiz. He speaks English. He's a very nice man."

"What am I supposed to do with Valdir?"

"He's looking for a guide to take you into the Pantanal by boat. It's an area of swamps and rivers."

"And snakes and alligators."

"Relax." Josh pointed to the bag behind the passenger's seat. "Open that."

It was made of brown leather. Nate sat it on his knee and opened it.

"Toys," he said.

"That's the latest cell phone. That's the latest computer. Look how small they are."

"Wow. And I'm supposed to use these in the middle of a swamp with snakes and alligators watching?"

"When you find her, I want to know immediately."

"What's this?"

"The best toy in the box. It's a satellite phone. You can use it anywhere on the face of the earth. Keep the batteries charged and you can always find me."

"Do the Indians have electricity?"

"Of course not."

"Then how am I supposed to keep the batteries charged?"

"You'll think of something."

In the crowded airport they drank weak coffee and read newspapers. Josh was very conscious of the bar; Nate didn't seem to be.

"Are you OK?" Josh asked.

"I'm fine. I'm not waiting for you to leave so I can run over to the bar and drink vodka."

"I'm not worried about you," Josh lied.

"Then go. I'm a big boy."

They said goodbye at the gate. At midnight, somewhere over the Caribbean, Nate fell asleep.

◆

The second plane descended and the pilot welcomed them to Campo Grande. Nate read his notes. Six hundred thousand people. A center for the cattle trade. Lots of cowboys. Rapid growth.

When he stepped from the plane, the heat hit him. Two days before Christmas and it was over thirty-five degrees.

He slept most of the hour it took to reach Corumbá. Set on the Bolivian border, the city had 90,000 people and was the capital of the Pantanal. River traffic and trade had built the city and kept it going. It was a lazy, pleasant little town. Storekeepers sat outside their stores waiting for customers and chatting with each other. Teenagers raced through the traffic on bikes. Children ate ice cream at sidewalk tables.

Nate's room at the Palace Hotel was on the eighth floor. There was a narrow bed, a desk with a chair, a small refrigerator with bottled water and beer, and a clean bathroom.

Nate stretched his tired body on the bed and went to sleep.

Chapter 4   Into the Pantanal

Valdir Ruiz was a pleasant man, happy with life in the way most Brazilians tend to be. He worked efficiently in his small office, just him and a secretary. He was proud of his English.

He produced a large air map and pointed to the Pantanal. No roads or highways. More than 100,000 kilometers of swamp. There were four red Xs along the western edge of the map, near Bolivia.

"There are tribes here," he said to Nate, pointing to the marks. "Guató and Ipicas."

"How large are they?" Nate asked.

"We don't really know," Valdir replied, his words very slow and careful. He was trying hard to impress the American with his English. "A hundred years ago, there were many more. But the tribes grow smaller. They have little contact with the outside world. Their culture hasn't changed for 1,000 years."

"Do we know where the missionaries are?"

"It is difficult to say." Valdir pointed at two of the Xs. "These are Guató. There will probably be missionaries around here. You must understand that there are at least twenty different American and Canadian groups with missionaries in Brazil. It's easy to get into our country, and it's easy to move around. No one really cares who is out there and what they are doing."

Nate pointed at Corumbá, then to the nearest red X. "How long does it take to get from here to there?"

"By plane, about an hour. By boat, from three to five days."

"Then where's my plane?"

"It's not that easy," Valdir said. He pointed. "These are cattle farms. Only a few can be reached by boat, so they use small airplanes. The airstrips are marked in blue. Even if you flew into the area, you would have to use a boat to get to the Indians."

"How good are the airstrips?"

"They're all grass. Sometimes they cut the grass, sometimes they don't. The biggest problem is cows."

"Cows?"

"Yes, cows like grass. Sometimes it's hard to land because the cows are eating the airstrip."

"Could I fly into the Pantanal, then rent a boat to find the Indians?"

"No. The boats are here in Corumbá. So are the guides."

"I'd like to fly over the area," Nate said.

Valdir rolled up the map. "I can arrange an airplane and a pilot."

"What about a boat?"

"I'm working on that. This is the flood season and most of the boats are in use. The rivers are up. I must warn you that air travel can be dangerous. The planes are small, and if there is engine trouble, well . . . There's no place to put a plane down in an emergency. A plane went down a month ago. They found it near a river, surrounded by alligators."

"What happened to the passengers?" Nate asked, afraid of the answer.

"Ask the alligators."

They walked to the window and watched the traffic. "I think I have found a guide," Valdir said. "He's a young man, just out of the army. He speaks English very well. His father was a river pilot."

Across the street was a small bar with three tables on the sidewalk. A red sign advertised beer. Two men shared a table with a large bottle of beer between them. It was perfect—a hot day, a party mood, a cold drink enjoyed by two friends.

Nate's head began to spin. His heart was beating fast and his breathing stopped. His hands shook. He could taste the beer. The slide was beginning. He took a deep breath. The moment would pass; he knew it would.

He thanked Valdir and left the office. He walked toward the river and found a small park. The late afternoon was humid; his shirt was stained with sweat and stuck to his chest. What happened back at Valdir's office had scared him. He sat on the edge of a picnic table and looked at the great Pantanal lying before him. A musician began to play his guitar as the sun sank slowly over the Bolivian mountains not far away.

◆

A pilot agreed to fly, but he wanted to leave early and be back in Corumbá by noon because it was Christmas Eve.

Valdir had hired a guide called Jevy. He was twenty-four, single, and strong. He ran into the Palace Hotel wearing a bush hat, shorts, black army boots, and a shiny knife in his belt. Nate liked him immediately.

His truck was old but ready for the jungle. They roared through the streets of Corumbá, slowing only slightly at red lights, completely ignoring stop signs. Jevy talked as he held the wheel like a race driver. Nate didn't hear a word. His heart stopped at each new intersection.

The airport was empty. The pilot's name sounded like Milton. He was friendly enough, but it was obvious he didn't want to fly or work on the day before Christmas.

"Do you feel safe?" Nate asked Jevy, when the pilot announced he was ready.

Jevy laughed and said, "No problem. This man has four small children and a pretty wife. Why would he risk his life?"

Corumbá was immediately beneath them. To the east and north a dozen small rivers spun circles around and through each other. Because of the floods, the rivers were full and in many places ran together.

In the west were the distant mountains of Bolivia. The sky was darker beyond the mountains. Milton dropped to 4,000 meters to stay below the clouds. He was worried about the dark sky.

"We'll watch it for a few minutes," Jevy said. Milton wanted to go home, but Nate at least wanted to see the Indian villages. He still held the faint hope that he could somehow fly to meet Rachel and take her back to Corumbá, where they could have lunch in a nice café and discuss her father's case.

Raindrops began hitting the windows of the plane, and Milton dropped to 3,000 meters. From over the mountaintops, the storm rushed at them. The winds hit the plane and it dropped suddenly. Nate's head hit the top of the cabin. He was very frightened.

"We're turning around," Jevy shouted.

Sweat covered Milton's forehead. The plane moved hard to the right. The sky toward Corumbá was black. Milton turned quickly east and said something to Jevy.

"We can't go to Corumbá," Jevy shouted. "He wants to look for a farm. We'll land and wait for the storm to pass."

Nate looked out of his window, and saw nothing, no nice little farms with long airstrips. The plane dropped 100 meters in less than two seconds. Milton pushed the plane down toward the ground. Thunder just above them sounded like a gun in a dark room and shook them to their bones.

Nate caught sight of a river, just below them, and he suddenly remembered the alligators. He didn't want to crash into a swamp.

Milton descended to 300 meters, where the ground could be seen in patches. Nate saw a white object below and shouted and pointed. "A cow! A cow!"

They had seen the airstrip too late to land with the wind, so Milton turned the plane to land in the face of the storm. Nate saw a boy with a stick running through the tall grass. And he saw a cow running away from the airstrip. He saw Jevy staring through the window, eyes wild, mouth open but no words coming out. They hit the grass. The wind lifted them into the air, and then they hit the ground again.

"Cow! Cow!"

The plane crashed into a large, curious cow and turned violently, all the windows bursting open, all three men screaming their last words.

Chapter 5   The Slide

Nate woke up, covered in blood. It was still raining. Milton and Jevy were lying on top of each other, but moving and struggling to get out of their seats.

Nate found a window and stuck his head out. The plane was on its side, with a wing cracked and folded under the cabin. Blood was everywhere, but it was from the cow, not the passengers.

The boy with the stick led them to a small stable. Out of the storm, Milton dropped to his knees and began to pray. They sat in the dirt for a long time, watching the rain, hearing the wind, thinking of what could have been, saying nothing.

Marco, the owner of the cow, appeared an hour later and began a heated discussion with Jevy and Milton about the value of the cow.

"I'll pay for the creature," Nate said to Jevy.

Jevy asked the man how much, then said, "A hundred dollars."

"Does he take American Express?" Nate asked, but the humor missed its mark. "I'll pay it." He'd pay as much as that to stop Marco complaining.

The deal was settled and the man became their host. When he

realized Nate was from the States, he sent for his wife and kids. They ate rice and black beans around a small table. The children sat on the floor beside the table, eating bread and rice, watching every move Nate made.

Marco had a small boat with a motor. The Paraguay River was five hours away. Maybe he had enough gasoline, maybe he didn't. But it would be impossible to get there with all three men in the boat.

Jevy had a plan. There was an army base on the edge of Corumbá. When the sky cleared, Nate carefully unpacked the satellite phone and turned on the power. The signal was strong, and Marco and his family gathered around. He wondered if they'd ever seen a phone.

Jevy called a friend who found phone numbers. He then explained the situation to an army officer and asked for help. After all, they had had a plane crash. Finally, the commander himself came to the phone. He and Jevy traded army talk for five minutes—places they'd been to, people they knew—then Jevy explained what had happened.

"No problem. A helicopter is ready. Give us an hour," the commander said. Milton smiled for the first time that day.

An hour passed. The sun was dropping quickly in the west; dusk was approaching. The army would not be able to rescue them at night.

It was Tomas, the youngest child, who heard the sound first. He said something, then stood and pointed. The sound grew louder, and they saw the helicopter. When it landed, four soldiers jumped down and ran to the group. Nate knelt among the boys and gave them each ten dollars. Then he picked up his bag and ran to the helicopter.

It was dark in Corumbá when they flew over the city half an hour later. They landed at the army base west of town, where the commander met them and received their thanks. He sent them away in a military vehicle driven by a young soldier.

As they entered the city, the car stopped in front of a small grocery store. Jevy walked inside and returned with three bottles of beer. He gave one to Milton, and one to Nate.

After a slight hesitation, Nate took off the cap. The beer was very wet and cold, and thoroughly delicious. And it was Christmas. He could handle it.

The first stop was the hotel. Nate went to his room, where he undressed and stood in the shower for twenty minutes.

There were four cans of beer in the refrigerator. He drank them all in an hour, assuring himself that this was not a slide. Things were under control. He'd cheated death so why not celebrate? No one would ever know. A few beers here and there. What was the harm?

♦

The phone woke him. His neck, shoulders, and waist were already dark blue—neat rows of bruises where he had hit the side of the plane.

"How are you?" It was Valdir. "Jevy said he thought you were OK."

"I'm fine, just a little sore."

"Very well. I have some good news. I rented a boat yesterday."

"Good. When do I go?"

"Maybe tomorrow. They're getting it ready. Jevy knows the boat."

"I'm anxious to get on the river. Especially after yesterday."

After Valdir hung up, Nate got up and moved slowly around the room. He saw the empty beer cans in the wastebasket. He would deal with that later. This was not a slide. He had nearly died yesterday and that changed things. Every day was a gift now.

Why not enjoy its pleasures? Just a little beer and wine, nothing stronger.

Nate dressed and walked into town. The stores were locked and the streets were empty. He went back to the park and looked down at the great Pantanal in front of him.

Somewhere in the vast wetlands before him was Rachel Lane. She would soon be one of the richest women in the world. How would she react to the news of her good fortune? The possible answers made him uncomfortable.

They had learned little about Rachel. Evelyn Cunningham, her mother, was from the small town of Delhi, Louisiana. When she was nineteen, she moved to Baton Rouge and found a job as a secretary in one of Troy Phelan's companies. She was a beautiful woman and Troy spotted her during one of his visits from New York. Within a few months, Evelyn was pregnant.

Troy's people arranged for Evelyn to go to a hospital in New Orleans, where Rachel was born in November 1954. Evelyn never saw her child. Troy arranged for the quick, private adoption of Rachel by a minister and his wife in Montana. Evelyn took ten thousand dollars and returned to Delhi. She moved in with her parents, rarely left the house, and began to miss her daughter.

She wrote letters to Troy, none of which were answered. As the years passed, Evelyn became more and more depressed. She killed herself on November 2, 1959, on Rachel's fifth birthday. She drove her parents' car to the edge of town and jumped off a bridge.

Rachel was an only child. Her adoptive father, Mr. Lane, died when she was seventeen. Troy reentered her life as she was finishing high school. Maybe he felt guilty. Maybe he was worried about her college education and how she would afford it. Rachel knew she was adopted but had never shown an interest in her real parents.

Troy met Rachel sometime in the summer of 1972. Four years later, she graduated from the University of Montana. Gaps appeared in her history after that. Nate suspected that only two people could tell him about the relationship. One was dead; the other was living like an Indian somewhere out there, on the banks of one of a thousand rivers.

Nate walked down the block. A car stopped next to him and Jevy leaned out.

"Let's go for a ride," he said. "I want you to see the boat. My father was a boat captain."

"Where is he now?" Nate asked.

"He drowned in a storm."

"Wonderful," Nate thought.

They stopped at the edge of the river bank to admire their boat, the *Santa Loura*.

"How do you like it?" Jevy asked.

"I don't know," Nate replied. The boat was at least eighty meters long, with two decks. It was larger than Nate expected. There was a small boat tied to the back which had paddles and a motor.

"No other passengers?" Nate asked.

"No. Just you, me, and Welly, the deckhand, who can cook."

Nate walked to the back of the boat, where there was a hammock.

"This is yours," Jevy said. "You'll have lots of time to read and sleep."

Nate sat carefully in the hammock, then swung around until he was fully inside it. Jevy gave him a push, then left to have another chat with the mechanic.

◆

Late in the afternoon, Nate stopped at a small store a few blocks from the hotel. He walked in to find a beer, maybe two. He was alone on the far side of the world. It was Christmas and he had no one to share it with. A wave of loneliness fell upon him and Nate began to slide.

He saw the bottles of alcohol, all full and unopened. His mouth was dry. He grabbed the counter and thought about Sergio back at the hospital and Josh and the ex-wives and the ones he'd hurt so many times when he crashed. Nate pointed at the vodka. Two bottles.

He walked back to the hotel. It would be dark in an hour, and Corumbá was gently coming to life. The sidewalk cafés and bars were opening, a few cars moved about. Nate went to his room, where he locked the door and filled a tall plastic cup with ice. He placed the bottles side by side, and opened one. He slowly poured the vodka over the ice, and promised himself that he wouldn't stop until both were empty.

Chapter 6   Legal Challenges

Next morning, Jevy drove to the river and parked near the water's edge. The *Santa Loura* hadn't moved. He was pleased to see that Welly had arrived. Welly wasn't yet eighteen, but claimed he could cook, pilot, guide, clean, and navigate. Jevy knew he was lying.

"Have you seen Mr. O'Riley?" Jevy asked.

"The American? No. No sign of him."

Jevy drove downtown to the hotel to find Nate. The girl at the front desk hadn't seen Mr. O'Riley. She phoned his room, and no one answered. Jevy persuaded her to give him the key.

The door was locked but unchained, and Jevy entered slowly. The first thing he noticed was the empty bed, then he saw the bottles. One was empty, and the other half-filled. He saw a bare foot, then stepped closer to see Nate, lying between the bed and the wall. Jevy gently kicked his foot, and the leg moved.

At least he wasn't dead.

Jevy pulled Nate up from the floor and rolled him onto the bed. His eyes were swollen and still closed, his hair wild, his breathing slow.

"Nate!" Jevy said loudly. " Speak to me!"

No response. In the bathroom he wet a towel with cold water, then wrapped it around Nate's neck. Nate opened his mouth in an effort to speak.

"Where am I?" he said, his tongue thick and sticky.

"In Brazil. In your hotel room."

"I'm alive."

"More or less."

Jevy carried Nate into the bathroom, into the shower, where he fell onto the plastic floor.

"I'm sorry," Nate said over and over again. Jevy left him there and went downstairs for a pot of strong coffee.

♦

It was almost two when Welly heard them coming. Jevy parked on the bank. There was no sign of the American. Then a head slowly lifted itself from inside the car. The eyes were covered with thick shades, and a cap was pulled as low as possible. Jevy walked to the passenger door and helped Mr. O'Riley out. He looked very sick, with white skin that was wet with sweat, and he was too weak to walk alone. Jevy almost carried him up the steps onto the boat where the hammock was waiting. He pushed him into it.

"What's wrong with him?" Welly asked.

"He's drunk."

"But it's only two o'clock."

"He's been drunk for a long time."

The *Santa Loura* moved away from the shore, and slowly made its way past Corumbá.

◆

Nate slept for four hours and the *Santa Loura* traveled slowly toward the north. The sun was beginning to fall behind the distant mountains of Bolivia. The air was light and much cooler.

"The water is high," Jevy said. "We'll go much faster on the return." He pointed to a place on the map. "The first Indian village is in this area. It will take two, maybe three days."

Nate didn't care. Time had stopped. His watch was in his pocket. He'd cheated death and so every day now was a gift.

"Are you OK?" Jevy asked.

"I'm fine. I feel good. This little trip will be good for me."

There was a lot more Jevy wanted to ask, but Nate wasn't ready to talk. He went back to his hammock with the papers Josh had given him. He put insect repellent on his arms and legs, and began to read.

◆

The courtroom filled with members of the Phelan family and their lawyers. At ten o'clock, Judge Wycliff came in. The room was silent as he took his place at the front of the court. "Good morning," he said.

Everyone smiled back. To his great satisfaction, the room was full.

"Is everybody here?" he asked. "I need to identify everyone. The first papers were filed by Rex Phelan."

Hark Gettys jumped to his feet. "Your Honor, I'm Hark Gettys," he said loudly. "I represent Mr. Rex Phelan."

"Thank you. You may take your seat."

30

Wycliff went around the tables, taking the names of the heirs and their lawyers. Six children, three ex-wives. Everyone was present.

"Twenty-two lawyers," Wycliff said to himself.

"Do you have the will, Mr. Stafford?" he asked.

Josh stood, holding a file. "I do."

"You represented Troy Phelan," Wycliff asked. "Did you prepare a will for him?"

"I prepared several."

"Did you prepare his last will?"

There was a pause. It grew longer as the Phelans leaned closer.

"No, I did not," Josh said slowly. The words were soft, but they cut through the air like thunder. The courtroom grew quiet.

"Who prepared his last will and testament?" Wycliff asked.

"Mr. Phelan himself."

"Oh my God," Hark Gettys said, under his breath but loud enough for everyone to hear.

"When did he sign it?" Wycliff asked.

"Moments before he jumped to his death."

"Did he sign it in your presence?"

"He did. There were other witnesses. The signing was also videotaped."

"Please hand me the will."

"What is this?" Troy Junior whispered to the nearest lawyer. The lawyer didn't respond. Fear seized the Phelans, but there was nothing they could do. Was the money slipping away?

Wycliff cleared his throat. "I'm holding here a one-page document that is the will of Troy Phelan. I will read it straight through."

He read the will. Even Ramble heard the words and understood them. Geena and Cody started crying softly. Rex leaned forward, his face buried in his hands. Mary Ross covered her eyes as her lawyer rubbed her knee. Her husband rubbed the other one.

The journalists were excited. They wanted to take notes, but they were afraid of missing a single word. Some couldn't help grinning.

Wycliff finished reading the document. He laid it down and looked around the room. The Phelans sat low in their seats. For the moment, all twenty-two lawyers were incapable of speech. Then they began to smile. They were going to get rich. Their clients were heavily in debt and had no choice; they had to fight the will. The lawsuit would go on for years.

◆

The head of South American Missions was a woman named Neva Collier. She'd spent eleven years working in the mountains of New Guinea, so she understood the challenges of the 900 people whose activities she organized.

And she was the only person who knew that Rachel Porter had once been Rachel Lane, illegitimate daughter of Troy Phelan. After medical school, Rachel had changed her name to wipe out her past. She had no family; both adoptive parents had died. She had only Troy, and she was desperate to remove him from her life. After completing the World Tribes training, Rachel had told her secrets to Neva Collier. Neva had promised never to tell anyone about Rachel, including where she was in South America.

Sitting in her small neat office in Houston, Neva read the extraordinary account of Mr. Phelan's will. She'd followed the story since the suicide.

Communication with Rachel was slow. They exchanged mail twice a year, in March and August. Rachel usually called once a year from a pay phone in Corumbá when she went there for supplies. Neva had spoken to her the year before. Rachel's last vacation had been in 1992. She had no interest in the United States. It was not her home. She belonged with her people.

♦

The lawyers met at a hotel, in a large room where the tables had been hastily put together in a perfect square. There were fifty people in the room. No Phelans were present, only their legal teams.

Hark Gettys started the meeting. He suggested that each lawyer briefly state his or her ideas about the lawsuit. Grit, the lawyer hired by Mary Ross Phelan Jackman and her husband, stood and demanded war.

"We must challenge the will. The old man was crazy. He jumped to his death. And he gave one of the world's great fortunes to an unknown heir. Sounds crazy to me. We can find psychiatrists who'll say he was crazy."

"What about the three who examined him before he jumped?" someone said from across the table.

"That was stupid," Grit said. "Phelan fooled you and you guys fell for it."

The head of the legal team for Geena and Cody Strong was a woman named Langhorne. She'd once been a professor at Georgetown Law School. Her lecture lasted ten minutes, and covered little new ground. Her conclusion was to challenge the will and hope for an out-of-court settlement.

Libbigail's lawyer, Wally Bright, was next. He had his own small company that usually handled quick divorces. He wore a dirty suit and a tie that was at least twenty years old. He had nothing prepared, no notes, no thoughts about what he would say next. He talked about injustice in general.

Two of Lillian's lawyers stood at the same time. One started a sentence and the other finished it. They repeated what had already been said.

The lawyers all agreed. Fight, because (a) there was little to lose, (b) there was nothing else to do, and (c) they would get paid by the hour for fighting. An hour passed before someone mentioned the contest clause in the will. The heirs risked losing what little Troy had left them if they contested the will. The lawyers spent little time considering this. They wanted to fight the will, and they knew their greedy clients would follow their advice. Not one brave voice suggested that the will be accepted.

They discussed Rachel, and where she might be. Should they try to find her? But they decided not to look for her because they couldn't agree what they would do if they found her.

The meeting ended on a pleasant note. The lawyers gave themselves the result they wanted. They left to call their clients and proudly report how much progress they'd made.

Chapter 7   Alligators and Indians

Nate spent the morning reading. Jevy joined him for coffee.

"So what do you think of the Pantanal?" he asked.

"It's magnificent. Were you born here?"

"I took my first breath in the hospital in Corumbá, but I was born on these rivers. This is my home."

"You told me your father was a river pilot."

"Yes. When I was a small boy, I began going with him. Early in the morning, when everybody was asleep, he would allow me to take the wheel. I knew all the main rivers by the time I was ten."

"And he died on the river?"

"Not this, but the Taquiri to the east. Five years ago he was guiding a boat of Germans when a storm hit them. Only the deckhand lived."

He was quiet for a moment, then he said, "A lot of people want to destroy the Pantanal. Big companies that own big farms. They are clearing large sections of land for their crops. The soil is not good, so the companies use chemicals to grow crops and the chemicals get into the water. They run into the rivers, the rivers eventually run into the Pantanal. Our fish swallow them and die."

"Doesn't the government help?"

Jevy gave a bitter laugh. "Have you heard of Hidrovia?"

"No."

"It's a big ditch. It will be cut through the Pantanal to link Brazil, Bolivia, Paraguay, Argentina, and Uruguay. It is supposed to save South America. But it will drain the Pantanal. And our government supports it."

Nate wanted to say something deep and serious about taking care of the environment. Then he remembered that his countrymen had destroyed large areas of the United States in the name of "progress."

"It's still beautiful," Nate said.

"It is. Sometimes I think it's too big for them to destroy. There is a small trading post a few hours away. We should be there before dark. Fernando is the owner, and he hears everything on the river. Maybe he will know something about the missionaries."

Jevy emptied his coffee cup and stretched his arms. "Sometimes he has beer for sale. I think we should not buy any." He walked away.

"Fine with me," thought Nate. A cold brown bottle of beer. Excellent beer. He began to sweat, though the sun was hidden and there was a cool wind. He buried himself in the hammock and prayed for sleep, a deep sleep that would take him past their stop and into the night.

He was wide awake when the boat stopped. There were voices, then a gentle bump as they docked at the trading post.

Nate swore he would remain on the boat. He would stay on the deck. The coldest beer in the world couldn't pull him away.

35

There was no such thing as a short visit in Brazil, but finally Jevy bought thirty gallons of fuel and started the engine.

"Fernando says there is a woman missionary. She works with the Indians." Jevy handed him a bottle of cold water. They were moving again.

"Where?"

"He's not sure. The Indians don't move on the river, so he doesn't know much about them."

"How far is the nearest settlement?"

"We should be close by morning. But we can't take this boat. We must use the little one."

◆

When the Portuguese explorer Pedro Alvares Cabral first stepped on Brazilian soil in 1500, the country had five million Indians. After five centuries of European "civilization," only 270,000 survived. It was a sick and violent history. If the Indians tried to live with the Europeans, they caught strange diseases and died. If they fought the Europeans, they were killed by weapons more deadly than poison arrows.

They were the slaves of ranchers and rubber farmers. Men with guns drove them from their homes. Priests murdered them, and armies hunted them.

Now the government was also the enemy. In 1967, the agency in charge of Indian affairs used chemical weapons to kill Indians. They gave the Indians clothing that was infected with diseases. Using airplanes and helicopters, they bombed Indian villages and land with poison gas.

In the 1990s, the government wanted to open up the region to the north of the Pantanal, but the Indians were still in the way. The abuse of Indians was growing as ranchers pushed deep into the Amazon, with the support of the government.

Nate read this sad history for four hours, then went to drink coffee with Jevy.

"Do you have any Indian blood?" he asked.

Jevy smiled. "All of us have Indian blood. Why do you ask?"

"I've been reading the history of the Indians in Brazil. It's pretty tragic."

"It is. Do you think the Indians have been treated badly here?"

"Of course they have."

"What about in your country?"

"Not much better, I'm afraid," Nate said. It wasn't a matter he wanted to discuss.

♦

It was still dark when the engine stopped and Nate woke up. Welly was loading the small boat. Three large gas tanks were arranged neatly in the center of the boat.

"These should give us fifteen hours," Jevy explained.

"How far away is the settlement?" Nate asked.

"I'm not sure."

Jevy packed a small tent, two blankets, two mosquito nets, some food, and bottled water. The last item he packed was a large knife.

"This is for the alligators," he said, laughing. Nate tried to ignore it.

Nate took the copy of the will, folded it, and placed it in an envelope. He wrapped the envelope in a piece of cloth, taped it to his T-shirt, and covered it with a sweater.

They waved goodbye to Welly. Mist settled just above the water, and it was cool. Since leaving Corumbá, Nate had observed the river from the safety of the top deck; now he was almost sitting in it.

They entered the mouth of the tributary that would take

them to the Indians. The water there was much calmer. On Jevy's river map, the tributary was called the Cabixa. It curled like string out of Brazil and into Bolivia, and apparently went nowhere.

Jevy slowed the boat as they approached the first fork. A river of the same size branched to the left. Which route would keep them on the Cabixa? But all the rivers led back to the Paraguay. If they took a wrong turn, the currents would eventually lead them back to Welly.

An hour later, they approached a little hut with a red roof. There were no signs of humans or animals.

"In the flood season, many people in the Pantanal move to higher ground. They load up their cows and kids and leave for three months," Jevy said.

"What about the Indians?" Nate asked.

"They move around too."

"Wonderful. We don't know where they are, and they like to move around."

Jevy laughed and said, "We'll find them."

Nate had completely forgotten about being eaten when they went around a bend and came close to a group of alligators sleeping in shallow water. The boat frightened and upset them. Tails moved and water splashed, but the reptiles didn't attack.

Two hours later, they entered a large lake with more than a dozen little rivers twisting into it. Jevy didn't know which one was the Cabixa. They saw a man fishing at the side of the lake.

When they were a few meters away, Jevy began talking to him. Finally, he said goodbye and they paddled away.

"His mother was Indian," Jevy said. "There's a settlement a few hours from here."

"A few hours?"

"Three maybe."

Nate moved lower in the boat and found a spot on the bottom between the box of food and the fuel tanks. The boat slowed. Engine trouble wasn't something he'd worried about. Suddenly Nate was really scared.

Then they were off again, the motor roaring as if nothing had happened. It became a routine; every twenty minutes, just as Nate was falling asleep, the steady beat of the motor would stop. Jevy played with the engine, then things would be fine for another twenty minutes.

The first sign of the settlement came seven hours after they left the *Santa Loura*. Nate saw a thin line of blue smoke rising above the trees, near the foot of a hill. Jevy was certain they were in Bolivia. The ground was higher and they were close to the mountains.

They came to a gap in the trees and saw two canoes. Jevy guided the boat to the bank. Nate quickly jumped out, anxious to stretch his legs and feel the earth.

"Stay close," Jevy warned. Nate looked at him. Their eyes met, and Jevy nodded toward the trees.

An Indian was watching them. A male, brown-skinned, bare-chested, with a grass skirt hanging from his waist, no visible weapon. He had long, black hair and red stripes on his forehead. He was very frightening.

"Is he friendly?" Nate asked without taking his eyes off the man.

"I think so."

"Does he speak Portuguese?"

"I don't know."

"Why don't you go find out?"

"Relax."

Jevy stepped from the boat. "He looks like he wants to eat you," he whispered. Nate wasn't amused.

Jevy spoke to the Indian, but it was obvious he didn't speak Portuguese. He looked young, probably not twenty.

There was a movement behind the Indian. Three of his tribesmen appeared. They weren't friendly folk; there were no smiles or hellos.

A young female suddenly appeared from the trees and stood next to the first Indian. She too was brown and bare-chested. Nate tried not to stare. She seemed to understand Jevy.

Speaking slowly, Jevy asked to see their chief. She translated his words to the men, who talked among themselves.

"Some want to eat us now," Jevy said to Nate under his breath. "Some want to wait until tomorrow."

"Very funny."

When the men finished talking, they reported to the woman. She told Jevy that they must wait by the river. Jevy asked if a woman missionary lived with them.

"You must wait," she said.

The Indians disappeared into the wood.

"What do you think?" Nate asked when they were gone.

"They catch diseases from outsiders," Jevy explained. "That's why they're careful."

They returned to the boat. Jevy cleaned the engine. Nate looked at the papers under his sweater. They were still dry.

"Those papers are for the woman?" Jevy asked.

"Yes."

"Why? What has happened to her?"

"Her father died a few weeks ago. He left her a lot of money."

"How much?"

"Several billion. He was very wealthy."

"Did he have other children?"

"Six, I think."

"Did he give them several billion?"

"No. He gave them very little."

"Did she love her father?"

"I doubt it. She was illegitimate. It looks as if she tried to get away from him, and from everything else. Don't you think?" Nate waved his arm at the Pantanal.

"Why did he leave a fortune to a child who didn't love him?"

"Maybe he was crazy. He jumped out of a window."

This was more than Jevy could understand. He looked at the river, deep in thought.

◆

The Indians were Guató, who preferred no contact with outsiders. They grew their food in small patches, fished the rivers, and hunted with bows and arrows.

After an hour, Jevy smelled smoke. He climbed a tree near the boat, and Nate joined him.

They could see the tops of three huts. Was he so close to Rachel Lane? Was she there now, listening to her people and deciding what to do? Would she send an Indian to bring them, or would she simply walk through the wood and say hello?

"What do you think they're doing?" he asked.

"Talking. Just talking."

"Well, we need to leave soon. We left the boat eight and a half hours ago. I'd like to see Welly before dark."

"No problem. We'll go back with the current. And I know the way. It will be much faster."

Back on the ground, Nate had settled into the boat to sleep when Jevy saw the Indians. They slowly approached the river behind their chief. He carried a long stick. It didn't appear sharp or dangerous.

The chief directed his comments at Jevy. "Why are you here?" he asked in Portuguese. His face wasn't friendly, but he wasn't aggressive.

"We are looking for an American missionary, a woman," Jevy explained. "We've come from Corumbá. This man is an American. He needs to find the woman."

"Why does he need to find the woman? Is she in danger?"

It was the first hint that the Indians might know of Rachel Lane.

"No."

"She is not here."

"Have you ever seen a woman missionary around here?" Jevy asked.

At first there was no response, then a slight nod. The man pointed, somewhere off to the north and west.

"She's with another tribe?" Jevy asked. "Guató?"

"Ipicas," the man said.

"How far away?"

"A day."

Jevy opened two maps and spread them on the ground. The Indians were very curious. The chief told Jevy that they hadn't come in on the Cabixa. They'd taken a wrong turn onto the River Guató. Jevy whispered the news to Nate. Nate was worried; he was trusting Jevy with his life.

The Indians talked among themselves. They couldn't agree on a route to get to the Ipicas. Finally, they turned again to Jevy.

"There is a settlement of Ipicas at the edge of the mountains," Jevy translated.

"How do we get there?" Nate asked.

"I think we go back to the *Santa Loura*, and go north half a day on the Paraguay. Then we use the little boat again to get to the settlement."

"Then what are we waiting for?" Nate asked, standing and smiling at the Indians.

Jevy said thank you to their hosts. The Indians offered food, which Jevy declined. He explained that they were in a great hurry because they wanted to return to the big river before dark.

It was almost 4 P.M. With luck, they could reach the Cabixa before dark. Welly would be waiting with beans and rice. As Nate did these quick calculations, he felt the first raindrops.

◆

The motor shut down completely after fifty minutes. The current kept them moving, but they went very slowly.

Jevy tried to fix the engine. He pulled the starter rope, as Nate said a prayer. On the fourth pull, the engine started, though not as smoothly as before.

"We'll have to go slower," Jevy said.

"Fine. As long as we know where we are."

"No problem."

The storm crept over the mountains of Bolivia, then roared into the Pantanal. Nate was sitting low in the boat, watching the river to the east, when he felt the wind. The rain suddenly fell harder. He slowly turned and looked behind him. The sky was dark gray, almost black.

Nate felt completely helpless. There was nowhere to hide. There was nothing except water around them, water in all directions. A strong wind swept in behind them, driving the boat forward as the rain hit their backs. Nate wanted to curl up and hide.

They came to a fork in the river, then to a meeting of rivers. They could hardly see through the rain. Nate was certain they were lost. Jevy quickly turned the boat around. Now they raced into the storm, and it was a frightening sight. The sky was black. The current was stirring up the river.

Just before dark, Jevy chose another small river, one of several. Then lightning came and for a while they could almost see where they were going. The rain wasn't so heavy. The storm was slowly leaving them.

"We should make camp," Jevy said. "We might get lost if we keep going in the dark."

"We've been lost for three hours," Nate wanted to say.

Jevy guided the boat to a bank and tied a guide rope to a tree. When the wind stopped, the mosquitoes arrived. Nate rubbed repellent on his neck and face, even his eyelids and hair. The mosquitoes were quick and vicious and moved in small black clouds.

Around 11 P.M. the sky cleared, but there was no moon. Nate tried his best to get comfortable. As he stretched his legs, his T-shirt rose slightly and a dozen mosquitoes attacked his waist.

Sleep was impossible.

Chapter 8   The Missionary

Flowe, Zadel, and Theishen, the three psychiatrists who had declared Troy Phelan sane, were fired. New psychiatrists were found. Hark Gettys bought the first one, at three hundred dollars an hour.

The heirs couldn't pay high hourly fees to the lawyers, so the lawyers agreed to take percentages of the final settlements. Hark wanted 40 percent, but he and Rex finally agreed on 25 percent. Grit squeezed 25 percent out of Mary Ross Phelan Jackman.

The winner was Wally Bright, who insisted on half of Libbigail's settlement. None of the Phelan heirs asked if they were doing the right thing. They trusted their lawyers. No one could afford to be left out.

Because Hark was the loudest of the Phelan lawyers, he caught the attention of Snead. No one had noticed Snead since the suicide. When the will was read, he was sitting in the courtroom, his face disguised with sunglasses and a hat. He'd left in tears.

He hated the Phelan children because Troy hated them. Over the years, Snead had been forced to do many unpleasant things to protect Troy from his families. And in return, Mr. Phelan left him nothing. Not a cent.

Over the years, the old man had made many promises to take care of Snead. He knew that he'd been named in one will. He'd seen the document himself. He would inherit one million dollars when Mr. Phelan died. At the time, Mr. Phelan was worth three billion, and Snead remembered thinking how small a million seemed.

He'd occasionally asked about the matter, but Mr. Phelan had cursed him and threatened to cut him out completely. "You're as bad as my children," he'd said to poor Snead.

Somehow he'd gone from a million to zero, and he was bitter about it. He would join the enemies simply because he had no choice.

He went to Hark Gettys' office. The receptionist explained that Mr. Gettys was very busy.

"So am I," Snead replied rudely. "Give him this envelope. It's urgent. I'll wait for ten minutes, then I'll walk down the street to the next law office."

The envelope held a note that read: "I worked for Troy Phelan for thirty years. I know everything. Malcolm Snead."

Hark appeared immediately, took Snead into a large office, and locked the door.

"So you worked for Phelan for thirty years," Hark said. "Were you with him when he jumped? Did you see him sign the will, the last one?"

Snead was prepared to lie. The truth meant nothing. What was there to lose?

45

"I saw a lot of things," he said. "And I know a lot more. This visit is about money. Mr. Phelan promised that he would take care of me in his will. There were many promises, all broken."

"Was he crazy?"

"He was or he wasn't. Doesn't matter to me. This is the way I see it. Since they're all heavily in debt, the kids have to contest the will. No jury's going to feel sorry for them. They're a bunch of greedy losers. It'll be a tough case to win. But you and the other lawyers will attack the will, and you'll create this huge lawsuit that gets in the newspapers. You don't have much of a case, so you hope for a settlement before you go to court. The size of your settlement depends on my information about Mr. Phelan's state of mind."

"What do you want?"

"Money. Five million."

"That's a lot."

"It's nothing. I'll take it from this side or the other. It doesn't matter."

"Any more witnesses?" Hark asked.

"Only one. Her name is Nicolette. She was Mr. Phelan's last secretary. She can be bought."

"You've already talked to her."

"Every day. We're a package. She's covered in the five million."

Hark closed his eyes and rubbed his forehead. "I don't object to your five million. I just don't know how we can get it to you. I need to think about this."

"I'm in no hurry," Snead said. "I'll give you a week. If you say no, then I'll go to the other side."

"There is no other side."

"Don't be so certain."

"You know something about Rachel Lane?"

"I know everything," Snead said, then left the office.

46

♦

At dawn the current was strong, so they moved with it as the sun rose. The only sound was the rush of the water.

"I guess we're lost, aren't we?" Nate said.

"I know exactly where we are."

"Where?"

"We're in the Pantanal. And all rivers run to the Paraguay."

Jevy tried to start the motor. On the fifth pull, the motor caught and then died.

"I'll die here," Nate said to himself. "I'll either drown, starve, or be eaten."

To their surprise they heard a shout. A kid of no more than fifteen came toward them in a tiny canoe. A long lazy conversation followed.

"What's he saying?" Nate asked Jevy.

"He says the Indians are not far away."

"How far?"

"One hour, maybe two."

"Can he take us there?"

"He may want a few dollars."

"Fine." The Phelan estate on one side of the table, and this little kid on the other.

"Ten dollars," Jevy said, after another brief discussion.

"OK." For ten dollars, they would be delivered to Rachel Lane.

They followed the boy in the canoe for twenty minutes until they entered a small shallow stream. It was almost one when they came to the higher ground.

The boy seemed afraid to go further. "Just up there," he told Jevy.

Nate gave him the money and they thanked him. The boy turned back with the current and disappeared quickly.

The river ran into a forest where the trees hung low over the water. Nate felt as if they were being watched. He waited for an attack of deadly arrows by Indians dressed in war paint and trained to kill anyone with a white face.

But they saw children first, happy little brown bodies splashing in the water. The mothers were bathing too. Jevy stopped the engine and began talking and smiling. An older girl ran away, toward the settlement.

Three men arrived within minutes. The oldest one said he spoke Jevy's language.

After a few minutes, Nate said, "Translation, please. What about the woman?"

"Don't rush it. I'm still trying to persuade them not to burn you alive."

More Indians arrived. Their huts were 100 meters away, near the edge of the forest. A little boy studied Nate. Very softly he said, "Hello." Nate knew they were in the right place.

No one else heard the boy. Nate leaned forward, and softly said, "Hello."

"Goodbye," the boy said. Rachel had taught him at least two English words.

"What is your name?" Nate whispered.

"Hello," he repeated.

Under the tree, the male Indians were talking.

"What about the woman?" Nate repeated to Jevy.

"I'm not sure. I think she's here."

They talked some more, then the Indians left—men first, then the women, then the children.

"Did you make them mad?" Nate asked.

"No. They want to have a meeting."

"Do you think she's here?"

"I think so." Jevy took his seat in the boat and prepared to sleep.

◆

They began to walk at about three P.M. A small group of young men led them away from the river, along the path to the village, then out again into the woods. They crossed another trail. Eventually they saw the first hut, then smelled smoke.

When they were 200 meters away, the leader pointed to a shaded area near the river. Nate and Jevy were led to a bench and left there with two guards while the others went to the village.

They wouldn't have brought them so far if Rachel weren't nearby. As Nate rested on the bench and stared at the tops of the huts in the distance, he had many questions about her. What would she look like? What kind of clothes would she wear? How long since she'd seen civilization? Was he the first American to visit the village? How would she react to his presence? And to the money?

Both of the guards were asleep when there was movement from the settlement. A group of men walked toward them, and Rachel was with them. Nate saw a light yellow shirt among the brown-skinned chests, and a lighter face under a hat. She was slightly taller than the Indians and carried herself elegantly. She could have been out for a walk among the flowers.

The Indians stopped, but Rachel kept walking. She removed her hat. Her hair was brown and half-gray, and very short. She was forty-two years old but she looked younger. She didn't shake hands, nor did she give them her name.

"My name is Nate O'Riley. I'm an attorney from Washington."

"And you?" she said to Jevy.

"I'm Jevy Cardozo, from Corumbá. I'm his guide."

She looked them up and down with a slight grin. The moment was not at all unpleasant for her.

"What brings you here?" she asked.

"I'm looking for Rachel Lane. My company has important legal business with her."

"What kind of legal business?"

"I can only tell her."

"I'm not Rachel Lane. I'm sorry."

Jevy sighed and Nate's shoulders dropped. She saw every movement. "Are you hungry?" she asked them.

They both nodded. She called the Indians. "Jevy," she said, "go with these men into the village. They will feed you and give you enough food for Mr. O'Riley."

She sat with Nate on the bench and watched silently as the Indians took Jevy to the village. He turned around once, just to make sure Nate was OK.

"Rachel Lane disappeared many years ago," the woman said, looking at the village in the distance. "I kept the name Rachel, but dropped the Lane. It must be serious or you wouldn't be here." She spoke softly and slowly.

"Troy's dead. He killed himself three weeks ago."

She lowered her head slightly, closed her eyes, and prayed. It was a brief prayer followed by a long pause. Silence didn't bother her.

"Did you know him?" she finally asked.

"I met him once years ago. No, I didn't know him."

"Neither did I. He was my father, but he was always a stranger. How did you find me?"

"Troy tried to find you before he died, but couldn't. He knew you were a missionary with World Tribes, and that you were in this part of the world. It became my job to find you. He had an awful lot of money. That's why I'm here. We need to talk business."

"Troy left me something in his will?"

"You could say that."

"I don't want to talk business. I want to chat. I was with a patient just an hour ago when the boys came to tell me that an American was here. I ran to my hut and started praying. God gave me strength."

"I thought you were a missionary."

"I am. I'm also a doctor. I changed my name after college, before medical school. That's probably when the trail ended."

A light wind came in from the river. She saw him glance at his watch. "The boys are bringing your tent here."

"We'll be safe here, won't we?"

"Yes. God will protect you. Say your prayers."

"Are these Indians friendly?"

"Mostly. But they don't trust white people."

"What about you?"

"I've been here eleven years. They accept me. There was a missionary couple here before me. They'd learned the language and translated the Bible. And I'm a doctor. I made friends when I helped the women through childbirth."

Jevy appeared with a group of Indians. One of them handed Rachel a small square basket. She passed it to Nate, who removed a small loaf of hard bread.

"We're staying here tonight," Nate said to Jevy.

"It's the best spot," Rachel said. "I would offer you a place in the village, but the chief must approve a visit by white men."

"I would like to leave by noon tomorrow," Nate said.

"That will also be the chief's decision."

"You mean we can't leave when we want?"

"You will leave when he says you can leave. Don't worry."

"Are you and the chief close?"

"We get along."

For a few minutes, Rachel watched as Jevy and Nate struggled with the tent. "I'm going," she announced. "You'll be OK here."

"What time do you folks wake up around here?" Nate asked.

51

"An hour before sunrise."

"I'm sure we'll be awake," Nate said, looking at the tent. "Can we meet early? We have a lot to discuss."

"Yes. I'll send some food in the morning. Then we'll talk. Say your prayers, Mr. O'Riley."

She stepped into the darkness and was gone.

Chapter 9   A Death

Next morning, Ayesh was walking in front of her mother when she felt the snake move under her bare foot. It struck below her ankle as she screamed. By the time her father got to her, she was in shock and her right foot had doubled in size. A boy of fifteen, the fastest runner in the tribe, was sent to get Rachel.

There were four poisonous snakes in their part of the Pantanal, and Rachel usually had the medicine to cure their bites, but she'd been unable to find the medicine for this type of snake during her last trip to Corumbá.

Ayesh was small and thin, and she'd probably die without medicine. Rachel prayed as she ran behind the boys.

♦

A group of Indians took Nate and Jevy into the village, where the chief wanted to see them. His wife was preparing breakfast. While they were eating, Jevy and the chief talked. After a few sentences, Jevy translated them into English.

Nate ate, listened, and watched the village for Rachel.

She wasn't there, the chief explained. She was in the next village looking after a child who'd been bitten by a snake. He wasn't sure when she'd return.

"He wants us to stay here tonight, in the village," Jevy said.

Nate wished he'd brought the satellite phone. Josh must be very worried. They hadn't talked in almost a week.

◆

Lawyer Valdir took the early call from Mr. Stafford.

"I haven't heard from Nate O'Riley in days," Stafford said.

"We have had many storms down here."

"You haven't heard from your boy?"

"No. They are together. The guide is very good. The boat is very good. I'm sure they are well."

They agreed that Valdir would call when he heard something from the boat. Valdir walked to the window and looked at the busy streets of Corumbá. There were many stories about people who entered the Pantanal and never came back. Jevy's father had piloted the river for thirty years, and his body was never found.

Welly found the law office an hour later. Valdir came out to see him.

"Who are you?" he demanded.

"My name is Welly. Jevy hired me to work on the *Santa Loura*."

"Where is Jevy?"

"He's still in the Pantanal. The boat sank. Jevy and Mr. O'Riley left in the small boat to find the Indians."

"When?"

"A few days ago. I stayed with the *Santa Loura*. A storm hit, the biggest storm ever. It rolled the boat over in the middle of the night. I was thrown into the water and picked up later by a cattle boat."

"Where was Jevy during the storm?" Valdir asked.

"Somewhere on the Cabixa River. I fear for him."

Valdir walked back into his office, closed the door, and returned to his window. Mr. Stafford was 3,000 kilometers away.

Jevy could survive in a small boat. He decided not to call Mr. Stafford for a few days. Give Jevy time, and surely he would return to Corumbá.

◆

During dinner Nate heard that the girl had died. A messenger arrived and delivered the news to the chief, and it swept through the huts.

As Rachel entered the village with her Indian assistant Lako, everybody stood and stared. They lowered their heads as she walked by their huts. She smiled at some, paused long enough to say something to the chief, then continued to her hut. She was tired and suffering and anxious to get home.

Lako found Nate and Jevy as the sun was falling behind the mountains. Nate followed the boy along the trail to Rachel's hut. She was standing in the door.

"I'm sorry about the little girl," Nate said.

"She is with the Lord." She sat outside the door. The boy stood under a tree, almost hidden by the darkness. "I cannot invite you into my home. Only married people can be indoors at this time of day."

"How long did it take you to get used to living here?" Nate asked.

"A couple of years. I missed home for three years, and there are times now when I would like to drive a car, eat a pizza, and see a good movie. But you adjust. I became a Christian when I was fourteen years old, and I knew that God wanted me to be a missionary. I put my faith in Him."

"Can we talk about Troy?" The shadows were falling fast. They were three meters apart and could still see each other, but the darkness would soon separate them.

"If you must," she said, her voice tired.

54

"Troy had three wives and six children that we knew about. You, of course, were a surprise. He didn't like the other six. He left them almost nothing, just enough to cover their debts. He gave everything else to you."

"I haven't seen Troy for twenty years."

"That's not important. He left his fortune to you. I have a copy of the will for you."

"I don't want to see it."

"And I have some other papers which I'd like you to sign, maybe tomorrow morning. Then I can be on my way."

"What kind of papers?"

"Legal stuff, all for your benefit."

"You're not concerned with my benefit." Her words were much sharper. "You don't know what I want, or need. You don't know me, Nate, so how can you know what's good for me?"

"OK, you're right. But it is very important for you to see these papers and sign them. All the heirs must tell the court, either in person or in writing, that they understand the will. It's required by the law."

"And if I refuse?"

"Honestly, I haven't thought about that. It's routine. Everybody always cooperates."

Rachel was quiet for a moment, then she changed the subject. "Do you have family?" she asked.

"I've had a couple. Two marriages, two divorces, four children. I now live alone."

"Divorce is so easy, isn't it? We marry, then divorce. Find someone else, marry, then divorce. Find someone else. The Indians never divorce."

"You've never married?" Nate asked.

"No. I thought I was in love once, in college. I wanted to marry him, but the Lord led me away. He wanted me here. The boy I loved was a good Christian, but he was weak physically. He would never have survived as a missionary."

"How long will you stay here?"

"I don't plan to leave."

"So the Indians will bury you?"

"Most World Tribes missionaries retire and go home. They have families to go back to."

"You'd have a lot of family and friends if you went back now. You'd be quite famous."

"That's another good reason to stay here. Money means nothing to me. You're part of a culture where everything is measured by money. People work all the time to earn money to buy things. They want to impress other people. It's sad. You're a very lonely person, Nate. I can sense it. You don't know God."

"I believe in God," Nate said, truthfully but weakly.

"It's easy to say that," she said, her words still slow and soft. "But saying is one thing, living is another. That boy under the tree is Lako. He's seventeen, small for his age, and always sick. Lako is the first to catch every disease. I doubt he'll live to be thirty. Lako doesn't care. He became a Christian several years ago. He talks to God all day long. He has no worries, no fears. If he has a problem, he goes straight to God and leaves it there. That little Indian has nothing on this earth, but he knows that when he dies he'll go to heaven. Lako is a wealthy boy."

Very gently, she touched Nate's arm and said, "You're a good person, aren't you, Nate?"

"No, I'm not a good person. I do a lot of bad things. I'm weak, and I don't want to talk about it. I didn't come here to find God. Finding you was hard enough. I'm required by law to give you these papers."

"I'm not signing the papers and I don't want the money. I'm sorry you came. You've wasted a trip."

Lako said something.

"He needs to go to his hut," Rachel said, rising to her feet. "Follow him."

Nate slowly stood. "I would like to leave tomorrow," he said.

"Good. I'll speak to the chief."

"I need thirty minutes of your time, to show you a copy of the will."

"We can talk. Good night."

♦

Josh met Judge Wycliff and showed him the video of Troy Phelan signing his testament. They watched the first part of the video without comment. It began with old Troy sitting in his wheelchair, being examined by the psychiatrists. The examination ended with the agreement that Mr. Phelan knew exactly what he was doing. Wycliff smiled to himself.

The room cleared. The camera across from Troy was kept on. Troy took out the second will, and signed it four minutes after the mental examination had ended.

"How are they going to sort this out?" Wycliff asked. It was a question with no answer. Rex and Libbigail had already started to contest the will. The other heirs would quickly do the same.

"What about the will he signed first?" Wycliff said.

"He didn't sign it."

"But I saw him. It's on the video."

"No. He signed the name Mickey Mouse. From 1982 until 1996, I prepared eleven wills for Mr. Phelan. The law says that with each new will, the old one has to be destroyed. When he signed the new one, we—Mr. Phelan and I—burned the old one. He enjoyed it. He'd be happy for a few months, then one of his kids would make him mad, and he'd start talking about changing his will. If the heirs can prove he wasn't sane when he signed that handwritten will, then there is no other will. They were all destroyed. His estate will be divided between all his children."

"Why would he give eleven billion to an illegitimate daughter who's a missionary? Sounds a little crazy, doesn't it? Do you think that Phelan was crazy?" Wycliff asked Josh.

"No. Strange, and very mean. But he knew what he was doing."

"Find the girl, Josh."

"We're trying."

◆

The next morning, Rachel spoke to the chief.

"He thinks there'll be a storm," she said to Nate when the meeting was over. "He says you can go, but he will not send a guide. It's too dangerous."

"Can we get back without a guide?"

"It wouldn't be wise. The rivers run together. It's easy to get lost. Even the Ipicas have lost men during the rainy season."

"I need to get back," Nate said. "This trip has already taken too long. We have to talk."

"I have to go to the next village for the funeral of the little girl. Why don't you go with me? We'll have plenty of time to talk."

Lako led the way. Rachel followed him, then Nate. He tried to persuade Rachel to take the money.

"If you had lots of money, you could buy lots of medicine. You could fill your shelves with all the medicines you need. You could buy a nice little boat to take you to Corumbá. You could build a hospital and a school, and spread Christianity all over the Pantanal."

She stopped and turned. "I've done nothing to earn the money, and I didn't know the man who made it. Please don't mention it again."

"Give it away. Give it all to charity."

"It's not mine to give."

"It'll be wasted. Millions will go to the lawyers, and what's left will go to your brothers and sisters. And, believe me, you don't want that. Those people will cause a lot of unhappiness if they get the money."

She took his hand. Very slowly she said, "I don't care. I'll pray for them."

They stopped by a stream for a few moments to rest.

"You said last night that you were weak," Rachel said. "What does that mean?"

"I'm an alcoholic," Nate replied. "I've hit the bottom four times. I have no money. I'm in trouble for nonpayment of taxes. I may go to jail, lose my license, and not be able to practice law. You know about the two divorces. Both women dislike me, and they've poisoned my children. I've wrecked my life."

"Anything else?" Rachel asked.

"Oh, yes. I've tried to kill myself at least twice. Once last August, then just a few days ago in Corumbá. I almost drank myself to death on cheap vodka."

"You poor man."

"I'm sick. I have a disease. I've admitted it."

"Have you ever confessed to God? He won't help you unless you ask. You have to go to Him, in prayer. He can forgive all your sins and you'll become a new believer in Christ."

"I don't know how to pray," he said.

She squeezed his hand. "Close your eyes, Nate. Repeat after me: Dear God, forgive my sins, and help me to forgive those who have sinned against me. Give me the strength to overcome temptations and addictions."

Nate repeated her words, but he was confused. Prayer was easy for Rachel because she did so much of it. For him, it was strange.

They opened their eyes but kept their hands together. There was an odd sensation as his burdens seemed to lift; his shoulders felt lighter, his head clearer. But Nate carried so much baggage he wasn't certain which loads had been taken away and which remained. He was still frightened by the real world. It was easy to be brave deep in the Pantanal, where there were few temptations, but he knew what waited for him at home.

"Your sins are forgiven, Nate," she said. "We'll pray again tonight."

"It'll take more for me than most folks."

"Trust me, Nate. And trust God. He's seen worse."

"I trust you. It's God who worries me."

She squeezed his hand tighter, and for a long moment they watched the water.

"I've been thinking about the funeral," Nate said. "I don't want to see a dead child. Jevy and I will go back to the village."

"Very well. I understand."

Chapter 10   Fever

The storm never came. When Rachel returned in the mid-afternoon, she and Lako went straight to the chief and reported on events in the other village. She spoke to Nate and Jevy. She was tired and wanted to sleep before they discussed business.

Later, she and Nate walked down toward the river, to the narrow bench under the trees. They sat close, their knees touching again.

"Every village has a local doctor," Rachel said. "He cooks plants and roots to make his medicine. He calls up spirits to help with all sorts of problems. These doctors are my enemies. I'm a threat to their religion. They attack Christians. In a village down the river, I had a small school where I taught reading and writing. It was for the Christians, but it was also open to anyone. A year ago we had malaria and three people died. The local doctor told the village chief that the people were sick because of my school. They were being punished. The school is now closed.

"The parents of the girl who died are Christians. The local doctor said he could have saved the girl, but the parents didn't call him. He blamed me for her death. And he blamed God. During the funeral today, he began dancing and singing. I couldn't finish the service."

Her voice cracked slightly, and she bit her lip. She couldn't cry in front of the Indians. She had to be strong all the time. But she could cry with Nate, and he would understand.

"I think you should go now," she said suddenly. "I think I saw a case of malaria in the other village today. Mosquitoes carry it and it spreads quickly. Trust me, Nate. I've had malaria twice, and you don't want it. The second time almost killed me."

It never occurred to Nate that she might die. If she died, it would take years to settle the Phelan estate. And he admired her greatly. She was everything he wasn't—strong and brave, happy with a simple life.

"Don't die, Rachel," he said.

"You're a good man. You have a good heart and a good mind. You just need some help."

"I know. I'm not very strong."

He had the papers in his pocket. "Can we discuss these?"

She read the will slowly. "Troy didn't care for his other children," she said. "I remember the day my mother told me about him. My father had just died. Troy had found me and wanted to visit. She told me the truth about my biological parents and it meant nothing to me. A year went by. He and my mother became friends over the phone. One day he came to our house. We had cake and tea, then he left. He sent money for college. He started acting like a father, and I grew to dislike him. Then my mother died. I changed my name and went to medical school. I prayed for Troy over the years, the same way I pray for all the lost people. I thought he'd forgotten about me."

He gave her the other legal documents. She read them carefully and said, "I'm not signing anything. I don't want the money. And I want you to do something for me. Don't tell anyone where I am."

This would be a huge news story: HUMBLE MISSIONARY IN JUNGLE SAYS NO TO ELEVEN-BILLION-DOLLAR FORTUNE. The journalists would come to the Pantanal with helicopters and boats to get the story. Nate felt sorry for her.

"I'll do what I can," he said.

The chief and some of the villagers came to watch them leave.

"You're sure we'll be safe in the dark?" Nate asked.

"Yes. The chief is sending his best men to guide you. God will protect you. Say your prayers. You're a good person with a good heart."

"Thank you. You want to get married?"

"I can't."

"Sure you can. I'll take care of the money, you take care of the Indians. We'll get a bigger hut and throw away our clothes."

They both laughed. Nate stood to say goodbye, and for a second he couldn't see. His eyelids began to ache. The joints at his elbows hurt.

Standing ankle deep in water, Nate put his arms around Rachel and said, "Thanks."

"Thanks for what?"

"Oh, I don't know. Thanks for creating a fortune in legal fees."

She smiled and said, "I like you, Nate, but I don't care about the money and the lawyers. Please don't come back. Just tell your people you never found me."

As they moved away, he waved at Rachel and the Indians. At the first turn in the river, he glanced over his shoulder. Rachel and the Indians hadn't moved.

He was sweating, even though it was cool. His arms and legs were wet. "I'm sick," he thought.

Jevy noticed him, and after a few minutes said, "Nate, are you OK?"

He shook his head no, and pain shot from his eyes to his spine. "Jevy, I think I have malaria."

"How do you know?"

"Rachel warned me. She saw it in the other village yesterday. That's why we left today. I have a fever and I can't see."

Jevy stopped the boat and shouted to the Indians. He quickly unrolled the tent. "You will feel cold and shiver," he said as he worked.

"Have you had malaria?"

"No. But most of my friends have died from it."

"What!"

"Bad joke. It doesn't kill many, but you will be very sick."

Moving gently, keeping his head as still as possible, Nate lay down in the center of the boat. Jevy spread the tent over him and secured it with two empty gas tanks.

The Indians were beside them. Lako asked Jevy what was happening. Nate heard the word malaria. Then they left.

Twice the canoes slowed as the Ipicas discussed which fork of the river to take. Jevy kept their boat 100 meters behind. He couldn't see Nate under the tent, but he knew his friend was suffering.

Lako was concerned about the American. "What should I tell the missionary about him?" he asked Jevy.

"Tell her he has malaria."

Nate heard their voices. The fever burned him from head to toe. His skin and clothes were wet. His mouth was so dry that it hurt to open it.

The storm followed them but didn't catch them. Jevy thought they would find Welly and the *Santa Loura* by dawn. The Indians were tired and ready to stop. Finally they found a spot and landed.

Lako explained that he'd been the missionary's assistant for many years. He'd seen lots of cases of malaria. He looked at Nate. A very high fever, he told Jevy. The fever would go away, but there would be another attack in forty-eight hours.

The oldest guide began talking to Lako. He translated for Jevy, telling him to keep in the center of the river. In two hours they would find the Paraguay. Jevy thanked the Indians and followed the moon to the Paraguay.

He arrived at the mouth of the Cabixa an hour after dawn. The *Santa Loura* was not there. Jevy went to find the owner of a nearby house, who told him about the storm that took away the boat.

"Where did it sink? What happened to the boy?"

"I don't know," the old man said. "He may be dead."

Nate wasn't dead. The fever went down, and when he woke he was cold and thirsty. He opened his eyes with his fingers. Every part of his body ached. There was a hot rash on his neck and chest.

"Where are we?" he asked Jevy.

"We're at the Cabixa. Welly is not here. The boat sank in a storm. Can you make it to Corumbá?"

"I'd rather just die."

"Lie down, Nate."

They left the bank and went on toward Corumbá. In the afternoon, they stopped at Fernando's store. Fernando looked at Nate.

"This is not malaria," he said, touching the rash on Nate's neck. "Malaria does not produce a rash like this. Dengue does. It's similar to malaria—fever, sore muscles and joints, spread by mosquitoes. You need to get him to Corumbá as quickly as possible."

It was almost two-thirty. Corumbá was nine to ten hours away.

Nate woke once, but couldn't see. He woke again and it was dark. He tried to say something to Jevy about water, just a small drink, but his voice had gone.

Rachel lay beside him under the smelly tent, her knees just touching his. He wanted to kiss her on the cheek. "When was your last kiss?" he wanted to ask her.

She was there to stop him dying. The fevers rose and fell. She patted his arm and promised he wasn't going to die. She tells everybody this, he thought. Death would be welcome.

The touching stopped. He opened his eyes and reached for Rachel, but she was gone.

◆

In Corumbá, Valdir called a doctor friend and persuaded him to meet them at the hospital. They raced through town in Valdir's car, ignoring lights and signs.

"Did you find the woman?" Valdir asked Jevy. "What did she say?"

"I don't know. I didn't really talk to her. I think she liked our friend back there."

Nate was curled tightly in the back seat, hearing nothing.

The doctor studied the rash, which began at Nate's chin and stopped at his waist. He was covered with mosquito bites.

"Looks like dengue fever," he said after ten minutes. Because he was a rich American, Nate got the best drugs in the hospital. The fever dropped a little, the sweating stopped.

"His temperature should fall soon," the doctor told the nurse. "I'll see him again early in the morning."

Nate was sleeping heavily when the nurse took him into a room with five other patients. He didn't see the open sores, the uncontrolled shaking of the old man next to him. He couldn't smell the waste.

◆

Like his father, Rex Phelan was good with numbers. He realized that six law firms were doing the same work. Six firms fighting the same fight, each wanting a big slice of the pie. It was time for the family to get together. He decided to begin with his brother T.J.

The two brothers met in secret. Rex began with the Snead story. "This is enormous," he said. "It could make or break our lawsuit. Snead will say he was the only person with Dad when he wrote the will. He wanted five million, but he only wants half a million now. We'll find some way not to pay him the rest. We have six law firms, all attacking the same will. And they all expect to get rich when we settle. How much are your boys getting?"

"How much is Hark Gettys getting?" Troy asked.

"Twenty-five percent."

"Mine wanted thirty. We agreed on twenty." Troy Junior was proud that he'd made a better deal than Rex.

"Let's play with numbers," Rex continued. "Imagine we hire Snead and he says all the right things. The estate wants to settle. We each get—maybe twenty million. Five goes to Hark Gettys. Four goes to your boys. That's nine, so we get thirty-one. But if we join up, then Hark will cut his fee. We don't need all these lawyers, T.J."

"I hate Hark Gettys. Why don't we fire him and stick with my guys?"

"Because Hark found Snead. This is a nasty business. Hark understands it. If we work together, he'll take twenty percent. If we can bring in Mary Ross, then he'll cut it to seventeen-five. Libbigail, down to fifteen."

"There's no sense fighting," Troy Junior said sadly.

"It'll cost us a fortune. It's time to make peace."

♦

Snead arrived for a meeting with Hark Gettys with a contract he'd written himself. Hark signed it and handed over a check for half a million. Snead examined every word, then folded it and put it in his coat pocket.

"What was the old man's state of mind the morning he died?" Hark asked.

Snead wanted to say the right thing. "He was out of his mind."

"How much time did you spend with him?"

"Off and on, twenty-four hours a day. I was on call around the clock."

"Who else did he spend time with?"

"Maybe young Nicolette, the secretary. He liked her."

"Did he have sex with her?"

"Would it help the lawsuit?"

"Yes."

"Then they had sex all the time."

Hark smiled. "Look, Mr. Snead, this is what we want. We need to know all the strange things Troy Phelan said and did. Sit down and begin writing. Talk to Nicolette, make sure they were having sex, listen to what she says."

"She'll say anything we need. How much time do I have?"

"We would like to video you in a few days. We'll hear your stories, ask you questions, then we'll coach you. When things are perfect, you'll be ready to talk to the judge."

Snead left in a hurry. He wanted to put the money in the bank and buy a new car. Nicolette needed one too.

Chapter 11   A New Beginning

It was the middle of the night when Nate finally woke up. He rubbed his sore eyes. His forehead was very hot. He was thirsty and couldn't remember his last meal. In the darkness of the room, somebody moved from bed to bed, finally stopping beside Nate's. She touched him gently on the arm.

"Nate," she whispered. "It's Rachel."

"Rachel?" he whispered.

"I'm here, Nate. God sent me to protect you."

He reached for her and she took his hand. "You are not going to die, Nate," she said. "God has plans for you."

He could say nothing. Slowly his eyes adjusted and he could see her. "It's you," he said. Or was it another dream?

He rested his head on the pillow. His muscles relaxed and his joints became loose. The heat left his forehead and face and he fell into a deep sleep. He dreamed of girls in white dresses floating in the clouds above him. They sang songs he'd never heard before, but they somehow seemed familiar.

♦

He left the hospital at noon the next day, against his doctor's advice. No one had seen Rachel at the hospital. Nate had whispered his secret to Jevy, who had asked the nurses. After lunch, Jevy began walking through town on foot, searching for her. No one seemed to know anything about a white woman arriving from the Pantanal.

In Valdir's office, Nate phoned Josh Stafford.

"The fever is gone," he said. "I'll come home in a couple of days."

"OK. Tell me about the woman."

"She's not interested in the money. You can't talk this woman into anything. I tried, got nowhere, so I stopped."

"Nobody walks away from this kind of money, Nate. Couldn't you talk some sense into her?"

"No, Josh. She is the happiest person I've ever met, perfectly content to spend the rest of her life working among her people. It's where God wants her to be."

"She signed the papers?"

"No. Sorry, boss. I tried to make her sign them. She'll never sign them."

Jevy found no trace of Rachel and he began to doubt his friend's story. Dengue makes you see things, makes you hear voices, makes you believe in ghosts. But he kept searching.

Nate also walked the streets. He saw the lights of a small church. That, he thought, is where she will be.

He stopped in the door and counted five people among the chairs. There was no one like Rachel. Three more people came in from the street. A young man with a guitar began to play and sing.

I need Rachel, Nate thought. The burdens I left with her have found me again. I need her to sit with me, to hold my hand and help me pray. Nate closed his eyes and called God's name. God was waiting.

With both hands, Nate gripped the back of the chair in front of him. He repeated every weakness and evil that attacked him. He confessed them all. He held nothing back. When he finally finished, Nate had tears in his eyes. "I'm sorry," he whispered to God. "Please help me."

He opened his eyes and wiped his cheeks. A voice was calling him, a voice from within. But Nate was confused. Surely God couldn't be calling him. He was Nate O'Riley—drunk, addict, lover of women, absent father, terrible husband, greedy lawyer.

Hurriedly, he left the church.

◆

Nate searched until the end of the week. He walked the streets, watched the crowds, checked out hotels and sidewalk cafés, and saw no one who looked like Rachel.

On his last day, he stopped at Valdir's office and collected his passport. They parted like old friends, and promised to see each other soon. They both knew it would never happen. Jevy drove him to the airport. He wanted to spend time in the United States, and asked for Nate's help.

"I'll need a job," he said.

Nate listened with sympathy, not certain if he himself was still employed.

"I'll see what I can do," he said.

The lady in the seat next to him on the plane ordered a beer. Nate studied the can. Not anymore, he told himself. He closed his eyes and asked God to give him strength. He ordered coffee.

Hours later, the plane dropped through the clouds. In Washington, the earth was covered with heavy snow. Josh was waiting for him.

"I thought you could stay at our place for a couple of days," he said.

"Thanks."

"How do you feel?"

"I'm fine. A little weak, that's all."

They rode in silence for a while. Traffic was slow. Then Nate announced, "I'm not going back to the office, Josh. Those days are over."

"Why?"

"Let's just say I'm tired."

Back at the house, he told Josh about his adventures in the Pantanal. He talked about Rachel and described her in great detail. He used her exact words when he talked about the money and the papers.

"If she won't take the gift from Troy's will, the money remains in his estate," Josh said. "If, however, the heirs can prove Troy was crazy, then there is no will. All seven of his children will share equally in his estate. If Rachel doesn't want a share, then her money will be divided by the other six. They'll get a billion dollars each."

"Why are we fighting for the will if Rachel says she doesn't want the money?" Nate asked.

"First and most importantly, my client gave away his estate as he wanted. I want to protect his will. Second, I know how Mr. Phelan felt about his children. He really didn't want them to get their hands on his money. I share his feelings—I hate to think what they'd do if they got a billion each. Third, Rachel could change her mind. We're going to fight, Nate. But Rachel needs a lawyer." He looked at Nate.

"You want me to be her lawyer?"

"There's no way around it, Nate. You have to take one last case before you leave. Just sit at the table and protect Rachel's interests. We'll go to Judge Wycliff and tell him you found Rachel, that she doesn't want to come to court. She's not sure what to do, but she wants you to act for her."

"We'll be lying to the judge."

"It's a small lie, Nate."

"I don't want to stay in town, Josh. Where would I go?"

"Take my house on Chesapeake Bay," Josh said. "We don't use it in winter. It's at St. Michaels, two hours away. You can drive in when you're needed."

Nate had to admit that it was a good plan. The lawsuit would never go to court. And he could earn some money for a few months.

"I propose a fee of ten thousand dollars a month," Josh said.

"Have you heard anything from the government about my tax?"

"The government will settle. You'll have to pay them a lot of money and they'll take away your law license for five years. But they won't do anything for a few months."

"Thanks, Josh." Nate was tired again. He wanted a warm, soft bed in a dark room.

♦

St. Michaels had a population of 13,000. There were stores on both sides of the main street, old buildings side by side. The house was on Green Street, and had a view of the harbor. The front yard was small and under almost a meter of snow. Nate parked his car and fought his way to the porch.

Inside, the house was neat and organized. Josh said a woman came every Wednesday to clean. But there was no coffee, and this was the first emergency of the day. Nate locked the doors and went into town. It was Sunday; all the stores were closed. Nate studied their windows as he walked along. Ahead, the church bells began.

Nate went into the church. It was a handsome building, but there were few people inside. Father Phil Lancaster, a little man with thick glasses and curly red and gray hair, stood at the front.

They struggled through the songs and prayers. Father Phil noticed Nate sitting in the last row and they exchanged smiles.

Sitting in the warm little church, safe from fevers and storms, safe from the dangers of the city, Nate realized that he was at peace. God was pulling him in some direction. He wasn't sure where, but he was no longer afraid.

As he left the church, Father Phil grabbed Nate by the hand. "Welcome," he said. "Welcome to Trinity Church."

"I'm Nate O'Riley, from Washington. I'm staying in the Stafford house for a few days."

"Nice to have you with us. When did you arrive?"

"This morning."

"Are you alone?"

"Yes."

"Then you must join us for lunch. My wife makes soup every time it snows. It's on the stove now. Please, our house is just behind the church." Phil was already pulling Nate's arm. "What brings you here?" he asked.

"It's a long story."

"Oh wonderful! Laura and I love stories. Let's have a long lunch and tell stories."

"Why not?" thought Nate. There was no food at the house.

At the back of the church, Laura was turning off the lights. Phil introduced her to Nate. She had short gray hair and looked older than her husband. She wasn't surprised to have a guest for lunch.

As they ate, Nate told them about his trip to Brazil. In his story, the storms grew fiercer, the boat smaller, the Indians less friendly. When he finished, the questions began. Phil wanted to know about the missionary—her faith, her work with the Indians.

It was almost three o'clock when Nate left. Phil would happily have sat at the table until dark, but Nate needed a walk. He felt as though he'd known them for years.

Near the harbor, he found a small store and bought coffee, soup, and cookies. There were bottles of beer by the counter. He smiled at them, happy that those days were behind him.

Chapter 12   A Letter to Rachel

Mary Ross fired Grit early Monday morning. Hark Gettys now had three of the four heirs from the first family. His percentage had dropped to seventeen-five, but the sum he could earn was enormous.

He called a meeting to tell the other lawyers. The back of Wally Bright's neck turned red with the news. He would kill Gettys if he tried to steal Libbigail.

"Stay away from my client," he said loudly. "We know the game you're playing. We're not stupid."

Snead came in and Hark introduced him to the group. "Now, the lawyers for the other side will ask you a lot of questions first. So for the next hour or so, assume that we are the enemy."

Hark began asking questions. Snead handled them well and relaxed. Then Ms. Langhorne asked Snead about the Phelan families.

"Did you know about Rachel Lane?" she asked.

"I haven't thought about that," Snead said. "What do you think?" he asked Mr. Gettys.

Hark was quick with the fiction. "I guess that you knew everything about Mr. Phelan. Rachel was ten or eleven when you went to work for Mr. Phelan. He tried to reach out to her over the years, but she would have nothing to do with him. So, if he left her everything, it shows that he was crazy."

Snead repeated and expanded the story. When he finished, the lawyers were pleased. They all began to help Snead find answers for difficult questions. For three hours they built his story, then for two hours they tried to tear it down. At one point, he was nearly in tears. When he was exhausted, they sent him home and told him to practice his answers.

Poor Snead drove home in his new car. He was determined to give them what they wanted.

◆

Nate planned to read and write through the morning. His plans were changed by a phone call.

"Are you busy?" Father Phil asked. "I'm at the church, working in the basement. I need some help."

Nate thought about the soup. There was plenty of it left. "I'll be there in ten minutes," he said.

Phil was measuring wood in the basement. "I'm building six classrooms for Bible study," he said.

It was a big job and Phil worked very slowly and took plenty of coffee breaks. As they worked, they talked. Nate talked about some of his troubles, including the problems with the government.

"What will you do?" Phil asked.

"I have no idea."

"Do you trust in God?"

"Yes, I think so."

"Then relax. He'll show you what to do."

For the next two days, Nate continued to help Phil in the basement. They made slow progress, but they became friends.

Nate was cleaning paint from his nails on Tuesday night when Josh phoned to call him back to the real world.

"Judge Wycliff wants to see you tomorrow," he said.

"What does he want?"

"He has some questions about your new client. I've told him you're Rachel's lawyer. You're needed. Meet me at noon at Judge Wycliff's office."

Nate put a log on the fire. He could put on a suit and tie. He could look and talk the part. He could say the right words, but he no longer considered himself a lawyer. Those days were over, thank God.

He could do it once more, but only once. He told himself that it was for Rachel, but he knew she didn't care.

◆

Judge Wycliff entered his office at twelve-thirty.

"Josh tells me you found the richest woman in the world," he said.

"Yes, I did. About two weeks ago."

"And you can't tell me where she is?"

"She begged me not to. I promised."

"Will she appear in my court?"

"She doesn't have to," Josh explained. "She knows nothing about Mr. Phelan's mental state, so she can't be a witness. We can proceed with the lawsuit without her."

"I need a letter from your client, saying that she's seen the will and knows what we're doing."

"Yes, Judge," Josh said.

Judge Wycliff began to ask questions about Rachel. Questions were dangerous. Wycliff mustn't know that Rachel didn't want the money. Josh interrupted. "You know, Judge, this is not a complicated case and everybody's anxious. Why can't we start the lawsuit as soon as possible? Get all the lawyers in one room now and make them produce a list of witnesses and documents. Then set a trial date for ninety days time."

"What about you, Mr. O'Riley? Is your client anxious to get the money?"

"Wouldn't you be anxious, Judge?" Nate asked.

And they all laughed.

That night, Nate began a letter to Rachel. He had the address of World Tribes in Houston. He would mark the letter "Private" and address it to Rachel Lane. Someone at World Tribes knew who and where she was. There must be some way to contact her.

He wrote the date, then "Dear Rachel."

An hour passed and he tried to think of words that would sound intelligent. Finally, he started writing about the snow. Did she miss it from her childhood? There was half a meter on the ground outside his window.

He told her that he was acting as her lawyer, and explained what was happening about the will. He told her about Father Phil, and the church and the basement. He was studying the Bible and enjoying it. He was praying for her.

When he finished, the letter was three pages long. Nate read it twice and thought she'd like it. If she received it, he knew she'd read it again and again.

Nate wanted to see her again.

♦

The story appeared in the newspapers on Friday morning. It said that Rachel Lane was acting through her lawyer, Mr. Nate O'Riley, to fight the people who were contesting her father's will. Mr. O'Riley had tracked down Rachel Lane, shown her a copy of the will, discussed the various legal issues with her, and become her lawyer.

The Phelan lawyers were astonished by the news. They met at Ms. Langhorne's office to discuss the case.

"We've seen nothing signed by this woman," Hark said. "No one knows where she is, except for her lawyer and he's not telling. It's obvious to me that she doesn't want to come forward."

"Lots of rich people are like that," Bright interrupted. "They want to keep quiet, otherwise everybody would be beating on the door, asking for money."

"What if she doesn't want the money?" Hark asked.

"That's crazy," Bright said as they all considered the impossible.

It's just a thought," Hark said. "If she doesn't want it, her share will go to the other heirs." The lawyers did some quick calculations. Eleven billion, less taxes, divided by six. Serious wealth was possible.

◆

The brown envelope was sent to the desk of Neva Collier, organizer of South American Missions. It was addressed: "For Rachel Lane, Missionary in South America, Personal." Inside was a letter, addressed: "To Whom It May Concern," and a smaller envelope. Neva read the letter aloud.

"Enclosed is a letter to Rachel Lane, one of your missionaries in Brazil. Please send it to her. I met Rachel about two weeks ago. I found her in the Pantanal. The purpose of my visit was a legal matter. She is doing well. I promised Rachel that I would not tell anyone where she is. She does not want to be disturbed with any more legal matters, and I agreed to her request.

"She needs money for a new boat and medicines. I will gladly forward a check to you. I want to write to Rachel again. Please let me know that you sent her this letter. Thanks. Nate O'Riley."

It wasn't easy to reach Rachel. Twice a year on March 1 and August 1, World Tribes sent packages to the post office in Corumbá. These included medical supplies, Christian literature, and anything else she needed. The post office held the packages for thirty days. If Rachel didn't collect them, they were returned to Houston. This never happened. Every August, Rachel went to Corumbá and called the World Tribes office. In March, the packages were sent up the river on a boat and left at a farm near the mouth of the Xeco River. Lako collected them.

In eleven years, Rachel had never received a personal letter. Neva copied Nate's phone number and address, then hid the letter in a drawer. She would send it in a month, with the usual supplies for March.

◆

Nate was in bed when the phone rang. A female voice said, "Nate O'Riley, please."

"This is Nate O'Riley."

"Good evening. My name is Neva Collier. I received your letter. I will send Rachel's letter to her."

"Thank you. I'd like to write to her again. Have you heard from her recently?"

"No."

Rachel had been in Corumbá two weeks earlier. He knew this because she'd come to the hospital. She'd spoken to him, touched him, then disappeared. But she hadn't called the World Tribes office? How strange.

"Why did you find her?" Neva Collier asked.

"You've seen the newspapers? You understand what her father did? Somebody had to explain what was happening and it had to be a lawyer."

"You mentioned some things she needs down there."

Nate told her the story of the little girl who died because Rachel had no medicine for the snake bite. "She can't find enough medical supplies in Corumbá. I want to send her whatever she needs."

"Thank you. Send the money to me at World Tribes. I'll make sure she gets the supplies. We have 4,000 Rachels around the world, and we don't have a lot of money."

"Are the others as special as Rachel?"

"Yes. They are chosen by God."

They agreed that Nate could send his letters to Neva and she would send them to Corumbá. If either of them heard from Rachel, he or she would call the other.

Back in bed, Nate thought about the phone call. Rachel had come to Corumbá because she knew from Lako that Nate was very sick. Then she'd left without calling anyone at World Tribes to discuss the money. It was very strange.

Chapter 13   The Lawsuit

The first stage of the lawsuit began on Monday, February 17. All the people who wanted to fight Troy Phelan's will had to declare their interest. Nate could question them to see if they were acceptable witnesses.

Nate didn't want to spend two weeks in a room full of lawyers. His attitude changed when he met the Phelan heirs.

The first witness was Mr. Troy Phelan Jr.

Nate introduced himself. "Are you currently under the influence of any drugs or alcohol?" he began pleasantly.

"I am not," Troy Junior said angrily.

"Which one is your lawyer?" Nate asked, waving at the crowd opposite.

"Hark Gettys."

The lawyers were annoyed. Nate hadn't learned which lawyers represented each client. It showed that he didn't respect them.

"How many wives have you had?"

"How many have you had?" Junior shot back.

"Let me explain something to you, Mr. Phelan," Nate said. "I will say this very slowly, so listen carefully. I am the lawyer, you are the witness. I ask the questions, you give the answers. Now let's try again. How many wives have you had?"

An hour later they finished with his marriages, his children, his divorce. Junior was sweating and wondering when it would end.

Nate used one question to lead to another. No detail was too small for him to investigate.

The afternoon was even harder. Nate asked about the five million dollars Troy Junior received on his twenty-first birthday.

"How was the money given to you?" Nate asked.

"It was placed in an account in a bank!"

"How did you get money from the account?"

"By writing checks."

He wrote a lot of them. Troy Junior never returned to college after he received the money. He simply partied. Nate revealed that Troy Junior didn't work for nine years. He played golf and football, bought cars, spent a year in the Bahamas, and lived in a grand style until his money ran out. Then he crawled back to his father and asked for a job.

Nate talked about what Troy Junior did after his father died. "You bought two expensive Porsches on credit. Now, two months later, you haven't paid a dime. You owe money for furniture. American Express wants more than fifteen thousand dollars. A bank is taking you to court because you owe them money. Correct?"

The witness nodded. They finally stopped at six o'clock. Ten minutes later, Troy Junior was in a bar two kilometers away.

The next day, they started again. Nate looked at Troy Junior and recognized the face of a drunk—the red eyes, the pink cheeks and nose.

He questioned Junior about the day his father died.

"You saw the psychiatrists examine your father? You missed nothing?"

"No, I missed nothing."

"Your family hired Dr. Zadel, correct?" For ten minutes, Nate questioned him about Dr. Zadel. He got what he wanted. Zadel was hired because he had an excellent reputation and was very experienced. Troy Junior admitted that he was pleased with Zadel, and had left the building believing that his father was sane.

"So why did you fire Dr. Zadel?"

"Because he was wrong. My father fooled the doctors, then jumped out of the window. He was obviously crazy."

"What would have happened if your father had signed the other will and not the handwritten one? And then he jumped? Would he be crazy?"

"We wouldn't be here."

Nate moved on to talk about the money Junior owed and his failed businesses. He finally freed the witness at five-thirty, day two.

He started the next day with Rex Phelan. Again, Nate asked hard questions about Rex's business deals. By noon of the following day, he'd revealed that Rex owed more than seven million dollars, there were a lot of court cases against him, and the FBI was investigating him.

During the afternoon, Nate talked about the five million inheritance Rex wasted. At the end of the day, the Phelan lawyers hoped that the worst was behind them—but they weren't sure.

Libbigail came in early on Friday morning. Nate asked about her five million and, under pressure, she told stories of good drugs and bad men. She now lived with an ex-biker and ex-addict called Spike.

"What would you do if you got one sixth of your father's estate?" Nate asked.

"Buy lots of things," she said. "But I would be smart with the money this time. Real smart."

"What's the first thing you would buy?"

"The biggest motorcycle in the world for Spike. Then a nicer house." Her eyes danced as she spent the money.

Mary Ross Phelan Jackman followed. The early questions

revealed that she took her five million and lived in Italy for three years. At twenty-eight she married a doctor and had two girls. It wasn't clear how much of the money was left. They lived well, but were heavily in debt.

Ramble came in after lunch. After a few questions, it was obvious that he was as stupid as he looked. He said that he seldom went to school, lived alone in a basement, liked to play the guitar, and planned to be a rock star soon. He played no sports, had never seen the inside of a church, spoke to his mother as little as possible, and watched MTV when he was awake and not playing his music.

Geena was the last witness of the week. Four days after her father's death, she and her husband had signed a contract for a 3.8-million-dollar house.

"How do you plan to pay for the home?" Nate asked.

The answer was obvious, but she couldn't confess it. "We have money," she said.

"Let's talk about your money," he said with a smile. "You're thirty years old. Nine years ago you received five million dollars? How much is left?"

She struggled with the answer for a long time, but finally admitted that there was only two hundred thousand dollars in her bank account. Her husband, Cody, had invested millions in bad business deals.

As Nate left the city that night, he thought about the Phelan heirs. He felt sorry for them, for the way they were raised, but he knew that in their hands the money would cause pain and unhappiness.

It was late when he arrived in St. Michaels, and as he passed the church he wanted to stop, go inside, kneel, and pray to God to forgive him for the sins of the week.

♦

The next day, Nate sat with Phil on the front steps of the Stafford house.

"I'm planning a trip," he said quietly. "I need to see my kids. I have two younger ones, Austin and Angela, in Salem, Oregon. My older son is a student in Evanston, and I have a daughter in Pittsburgh."

"When did you see them last?"

"It's over a year since I saw Daniel and Kaitlin, the two from my first marriage. I took the two younger ones to a ball game last July. I got drunk and don't remember driving back home."

"Do you expect the trip to be successful?" Phil asked.

"I'm not sure what to expect. I want to hold my kids and apologize for being such a bad father, but I'm not sure how that's supposed to help them now."

"You can't keep on blaming yourself, Nate. You're allowed to forget the past. God certainly has. Show your kids what you are now."

Later, long after Phil had gone home, Nate sat by the fire and began another letter to Rachel. It was his third. "Dear Rachel," he began, "I have just spent a very unpleasant week with your brothers and sisters." He told her he was sending a check to World Tribes for five thousand dollars for a boat and medical supplies. A lot of good things, he informed her, could be done with her inheritance.

♦

At eight-thirty on Tuesday morning, Snead came into the courtroom. The lawyers had been coaching him for weeks. It was important that the judge believed his stories.

Josh had known Snead for many years. Mr. Phelan often talked about getting rid of him. Josh guessed that he was being paid to

84

give evidence, and had discovered that Snead now had an expensive apartment and a new car.

Snead was ready. If Nate asked him whether he was being paid to appear, Snead would lie about the half a million dollars he had already received and the promise of a further four and a half million.

Nate introduced himself, and then asked loudly, "Mr. Snead, how much are you being paid to give evidence in this case?"

Snead thought the question would be, "Are you being paid?" not, "How much?" He looked wildly at Hark Gettys. Mr. O'Riley seemed to know everything.

The Phelan lawyers shrank in their seats.

"How much are you being paid?" Nate asked again.

"Five hundred thousand dollars," Snead admitted.

"Have you already received this money?"

Snead didn't know whether to lie or tell the truth, so he said, "Yes."

"Half a million now, how much later?" Nate asked.

Anxious to start lying, Snead answered, "Nothing."

"Who paid you this money?"

"The lawyers for the Phelan heirs."

"Did you go to them, or did they go to you?"

"I went to them." Finally, Snead was on familiar territory. "I was with Mr. Phelan before he died and I knew the poor man was out of his mind."

"How long did you work for Mr. Phelan?"

"Thirty years."

"And you knew everything about him, right?"

"Yes."

"And you didn't tell anyone that he was crazy?"

Snead thought he was doing well. "It was a private matter."

"Until now. Until they offered you half a million dollars, right?"

Snead could not think of a quick reply.

"In the last fourteen years of his life, Mr. Phelan wrote eleven wills. In one of them, he left you a million dollars. Did you tell anyone then that he was crazy?"

"It wasn't my job to tell."

Nate continued to question him. Late in the afternoon he suddenly asked, "Did you sign a contract with the lawyers when you took the half a million?"

A simple no would have been enough, but Snead hesitated, looked at Hark, and then looked at Nate.

"Uh, of course not," he said. Nobody believed him.

♦

Nicolette, the secretary, lasted for eight minutes. She was twenty-three, with few qualifications except for a nice chest, a pretty face, and blond hair.

Nate asked, "Did you ever have sex with Mr. Phelan."

She tried to look embarrassed, but said yes anyway.

"For how long?"

"Usually ten minutes."

"No, I mean for how long a period of time? Starting in what month and ending when?"

"Oh, I only worked there for five months."

"Did Mr. Phelan have any marks on his body?"

Any of the Phelan wives could have told the lawyers that Troy had a purple mark the size of a silver dollar at the top of his right leg. Nobody had asked.

"Not that I recall," Nicolette answered.

"No further questions," Nate said.

Nicolette left the room and Nate slid a photo across the table to his enemies. It was a picture of Troy Phelan's body. Nate didn't say a word, didn't need to. The mark stared out from the photo.

Chapter 14   The Settlement

At the end of the week, Nate left the city. He was exhausted from nine days of questioning the Phelan heirs. He felt ashamed. He pitied the Phelan children. He felt sorry for Snead, a sad little man who just wanted to survive.

Two days later Nate arrived in Salem, where his kids from his second marriage lived with their mother, Christi, and her new husband, Theo. The last time he saw them, Nate was drunk and fought with his ex-wife in the front yard while the children watched. Theo had threatened him with a shovel. Nate later woke up in his car, in the parking lot of a McDonald's, with six empty beer cans on the seat beside him.

He called Christi four hours before he arrived at their home.

"Christi, it's me, Nate," he said. "I'm in Oregon. I'd like to see the kids maybe tonight, tomorrow."

"Well, sure, Nate. I guess we can work something out. But the kids are very busy, you know, school, dance class, soccer."

"How are they?"

"They're doing very well. We love Oregon."

They agreed to have dinner the following night. That gave her enough time to prepare the kids. Theo decided to work late.

Nate kissed Angela. Austin just shook hands. Christi stayed in her bedroom for an hour while their father got to know his children again.

Dinner lasted an hour. At seven o'clock, Nate said he had to go. "I have a soccer game tomorrow, Dad," Austin said, and Nate's heart almost stopped. He couldn't remember the last time he'd been called Dad.

"It's at the school," Angela said. "Could you come?"

Nate didn't know what to say. Christi settled the issue. "I'll be there. We could talk," she said.

"Of course, I'll come," he said. The children kissed him. Driving away, Nate suspected Christi wanted to see him two days in a row to examine his eyes. She knew the signs.

Nate stayed in Salem for three days. He watched his son play soccer and was full of pride. He was invited back to dinner, but agreed to come only if Theo joined them. He had lunch with Angela and her friends at school.

He left Salem with a broken heart. How could a man lose such a wonderful family? He remembered almost nothing about the kids when they were smaller—no school plays, Christmas mornings, trips to the mall. Now they were almost grown, and another man was raising them.

♦

While Nate drove through Montana, Hark Gettys sent more papers to the court. There was no word from Rachel Lane. She obviously had no interest in the lawsuit. Didn't she want the money? It was a crazy idea—but why hadn't she appeared in court?

The heirs couldn't win. They had to find a reason to settle. Rachel Lane's lack of interest was a very good reason.

♦

Daniel, his oldest child, met Nate in a bar near the university. He was waiting with a girl. Both were smoking and had bottles in front of them.

"This is Stef," Daniel said. "She's a model."

The first thing Nate noticed about Stef was her gray lipstick, applied heavily to her thick lips. She was certainly thin enough to be a model. Nate disliked her immediately.

"You want a beer?" Daniel asked.

"No, just water," Nate said. Daniel shouted at the waiter.

"How's school?" Nate asked.

"I dropped out." Daniel was angry and tense. The girl was there for two reasons. She would prevent hasty words and a fight. Nate suspected that his son had no money, that he wanted to punish his father for lack of support. He was afraid, though, because Nate was weak and might start to slide again. Stef would keep a hold on his anger and his language. The second reason was to make the meeting as short as possible.

"Why did you drop out of school?" Nate asked.

"It was boring."

"He ran out of money," Stef said helpfully.

Nate wanted to pull out his checkbook and solve the kid's problems. That's what he'd always done. But now Daniel was twenty-three and it was time for him to sink or swim on his own.

"It's good for you," Nate said. "Work for a while. It'll make you appreciate school."

After four drinks, Stef was drunk, and Daniel and Nate had nothing else to say. He wrote down his phone number at St. Michaels and gave it to Daniel. "This is where I'll be for the next couple of months. Call me if you need me."

"See you," Daniel said.

"Take care."

♦

Two days later, he was in Pittsburgh for his third and final meeting with his children. It didn't happen. He'd spoken twice to Kaitlin, and the details were clear. She said she'd meet him for dinner at seven-thirty, at the restaurant in his hotel. She called him at eight-thirty and said that a friend had been involved in an accident. She was at the hospital.

Nate suggested that they have lunch the following day. Kaitlin said that she couldn't. Her friend had a head injury, and she planned to stay with her until she was stable. She couldn't see Nate. She couldn't leave the hospital.

Did she hate him so much? In a lonely hotel room, in a city where he knew no one, it was easy to pity himself. He grabbed the phone and got busy. He called Phil to check on things at St. Michaels. He called Sergio. He felt surprisingly under control. His hotel room had a minibar, and he hadn't been near it.

He called Josh. "You need to come home, Nate," Josh said. "I have a plan."

◆

Nate wasn't invited to the peace talks. Josh wanted to gain the trust of the Phelan lawyers. His plan was to meet with Hark and the others, then with Nate, until they struck a deal. The Phelan lawyers dreamed of a quick settlement. They believed they would become millionaires.

Josh began by giving his opinion that the lawyers couldn't win their lawsuit. Troy Phelan's will was legal. Phelan's children and ex-wives had carefully chosen the three psychiatrists. He talked about Rachel Lane as if he'd known her for years. She was a wonderful lady who lived a very simple life in another country. She didn't understand legal matters and didn't want a fight. And she'd been closer to Troy than most people knew.

"What does Rachel Lane plan to do with the money?" one of the lawyers asked.

"I'm not sure," Josh said, as if he and Rachel discussed it every day. "She'll probably keep a little, and give most of it to charity. In my opinion, that's what Troy wanted. He knew that if your clients got the money, it wouldn't last ninety days. By leaving it to Rachel, he knew it would be passed on to people in need."

"We can take this lawsuit to the highest courts," Langhorne said. "Does she realize this could take years?"

"She does," Josh said. "That's why she would like to discuss settlement possibilities."

"Where do we start?" asked Wally Bright.

For a long time, they talked numbers. Then Josh said, "Nate O'Riley has contacted his client. She will offer each of the six heirs ten million dollars."

The lawyers made rapid calculations. Hark had three clients; 17.5 percent gave him a fee of 5.25 million. Wally Bright would collect five million from his contract with Libbigail and Spike. The other lawyers would collect two million.

Wally spoke first. "My client will settle for no less than fifty million." The others shook their heads too, and tried to look disgusted at Josh's offer.

They talked about numbers for a while, then Josh said, "Rachel Lane is not a greedy woman. I think she might settle at twenty million per heir."

The lawyers' fees doubled—over ten million for Hark alone. Poor Wally, at ten million now, suddenly felt sick and asked to leave the meeting.

◆

Nate was helping Father Phil when the phone rang. It was Josh.

"It couldn't have gone better. I stopped at twenty million, they want fifty."

"Fifty?" Nate said in disbelief.

"Yes, but they're already spending the money. I bet two of them are at the Mercedes garage right now. We should complete the deal on Wednesday."

"I can't wait," Nate said.

Time for a coffee break. "We meet the judge on Wednesday,"

Nate told Phil. "Then I'm going back to the Pantanal to tell Rachel what's happened."

"Are you excited?"

"I don't know. I want to see her, but I'm not sure she wants to see me. She's very happy and she doesn't want any part of this world."

"Then why do it?"

"Because if she rejects the money again, the other side gets everything."

"But you've already said that Rachel won't take the money. She's not going to change her mind," Phil said.

"No. Never."

"So the trip down is a waste of time?"

"I'm afraid so. But at least we'll try."

♦

All the Phelan heirs were in the courtroom except for Ramble. Judge Wycliff explained that the purpose of the meeting was to explore a settlement. He made it clear that he didn't think the Phelan lawyers had much of a case. He asked Josh to tell him about the earlier settlement meeting on Monday.

"I want to know exactly where we are," he said.

Josh was brief. The heirs wanted fifty million dollars each. Rachel was offering twenty million to settle.

Nate was bored. It would be fun to stand up and tell them that Rachel wasn't offering any money to settle, and run out of the room. They would sit in shock for a few seconds, then they would chase him like hungry dogs.

When Josh finished, Hark began to speak. He talked about the Phelan children and their problems, admitting that they were rich and spoiled. Their father didn't care for them and they hadn't learned the normal lessons children learn from their parents.

They made many mistakes when they received five million dollars on their twenty-first birthdays. Now they knew better. Hark spoke well, and when he sat down the room was silent.

The lawyers thought Nate controlled the money. He could fight them for an hour or two, try to offer less than the fifty million. But he wasn't in the mood.

"My client will agree to fifty million," he said.

"Well, then," Wycliff asked. "Do we have a deal?"

Out of habit, the Phelan lawyers put their heads together. They grouped around Hark and tried to whisper, but words failed them.

"It's a deal," Hark announced, twenty-six million dollars richer.

Rachel had to sign and approve the settlement. Nate said that it would take a few days for him to get the signature.

Chapter 15　Return to the Pantanal

On Friday afternoon, Phil drove Nate to the Baltimore–Washington airport. In nine hours he would be in Corumbá.

He and Josh had written a trust document for Rachel. The money she received would be placed in a trust, named the Rachel Trust. The money itself wouldn't be touched, but the trustees could invest it and use the profits for charity work. If Rachel wanted, she would never see or touch the money. It would take only a quick signature and the Phelan estate would be closed. If she didn't agree to sign, then she must write a letter to say that she didn't want the money. She could decline the gift, but she had to tell the court. The law would then give the money to the Phelan children.

How would she react when he arrived? He hoped that she

would be delighted to see him, but he wasn't sure. He remembered her waving to his boat as he left. She was standing among her people, waving him away, saying goodbye forever. She didn't want to be bothered with the things of the world.

◆

Valdir had hired a helicopter which took him to the trading post in the Pantanal. His old friends Jevy and Welly were waiting for him on the ground.

Time was precious. Nate feared storms, darkness, floods, and mosquitoes, and he wanted to move as quickly as possible. Nate and Jevy quickly climbed into the boat and set off. Jevy thought it would take them three hours to reach the Indian settlement.

The trees on both sides of the river grew thicker, and Nate began to recognize the territory. Finally, they stepped off the boat where Rachel had waved goodbye. A young Indian ran toward them. He told them to stay there, by the river, until further orders. He seemed scared.

As they waited, Jevy talked about his efforts to find Rachel in Corumbá. "I tell you," he said, "I have listened to people on the river and the lady did not come. She was not in the hospital. You were dreaming, my friend."

Nate didn't want to argue. He wasn't sure himself.

A mosquito circled Nate's hand. He wanted to crush it, but instead he waited. Would his superrepellent work? His ears, neck, and face were covered in oil. The mosquito made a sudden dive toward the back of his hand, then stopped. It pulled away and disappeared. A second attack of dengue would probably kill him. Nate wasn't taking any chances.

Nate watched the village. He expected to see Rachel move elegantly between the huts and along the path to greet them. By now she knew the white man was back.

They saw the chief walking slowly toward them, followed by an Ipica who Nate recognized. They stopped about twenty meters from the bench. They weren't smiling; in fact, the chief looked very unpleasant. In Portuguese, he asked, "What do you want?"

"Tell him we want to see the missionary," Nate said, and Jevy translated.

"Why?" came the reply.

Nate remembered the chief as a man with a quick smile and a big laugh. Now his face had little expression. His eyes looked hard. He stood as far away from them as possible. Something was wrong. Something had changed.

He told them to wait, then left again and went back to the village. Half an hour passed. By now Rachel knew who they were; the chief would have told her. And she wasn't coming to meet them.

When the chief came back, he was alone. They followed him for fifty meters, then moved behind the huts on another trail. Nate could see the area around the village. It was empty; there was not a single Ipica walking about. No children were playing. No women were cooking and cleaning. There was no sound. The only movement was the smoke from their fires.

Then he saw faces at the windows. They were being watched. The chief kept them away from the huts as if they were carrying diseases. He turned onto another trail, one that led through the woods for a few moments. When they came to the end of it, they were near Rachel's hut.

There was no sign of her. The chief led them past the front door and to the side. Under the thick shade of the trees, they saw the graves.

The matching white crosses were made of wood. They were small and stuck into the fresh dirt at the far end of both graves.

The chief began talking.

"The woman is on the left; Lako is on the right," Jevy translated. "Malaria has killed ten people since we left."

The chief went on talking. Nate looked at the pile of dirt on the left. Rachel Lane was buried there, the bravest person he'd ever known because she had no fear of death. She welcomed it. She was at peace, her soul finally with God, her body lying forever among the people she loved.

She wouldn't want anyone to be sad. She wouldn't approve of tears, and Nate had none to give her. He'd hardly known her, but his heart ached anyway. He'd thought about her every day since he left the Pantanal. He'd dreamed about her, felt her touch, heard her voice, remembered her wisdom. She'd taught him to pray and given him hope. He'd never met anyone like Rachel Lane and he missed her greatly.

"The chief says we can't stay long," Jevy said. "The spirits blame us for the malaria. It arrived when we came the first time. They are not happy to see us. He has something to show you."

Slowly Nate followed the chief into Rachel's hut. The chief pointed to a box on a small table.

"There are things in that box for you," Jevy translated.

"For me?"

"Yes. She knew she was dying. She asked the chief to guard her hut. If the American came, then show him the box."

Inside the box there were three letters from World Tribes. Nate didn't read them because at the bottom of the box he saw her will. On it, she had written: "Last Testament of Rachel Lane Porter."

It read:

I, Rachel Lane Porter, child of God, resident of His world, citizen of the United States, am sane and healthy. This is my last testament.

1. This is my first and last will. Every word is written by my hand.

2. I have a copy of the last testament of my father, Troy Phelan, dated December 9, 1996. He left me most of his fortune.

3. I do not reject any of Troy Phelan's estate. Nor do I want to receive it. Place it in a trust.

4. The income from the trust can be used to: a) continue the work of World Tribes missionaries around the world, b) spread the word of Christ, c) protect the native people in Brazil and South America, d) feed the hungry, heal the sick, shelter the homeless, and save the children.

5. I appoint my friend Nate O'Riley to manage the trust. Signed, the sixth day of January 1997, at Corumbá, Brazil.

RACHEL LANE PORTER

There was a second letter, typed and written in Portuguese.

Nate read the will again. January 6 was the day he walked out of the hospital in Corumbá. She wasn't a dream. She'd touched him and told him he wouldn't die. Then she'd written her will.

Nate gave the second letter to Jevy and told him to read it.

"It's from a lawyer," Jevy said. "He says he saw Rachel Lane Porter sign her testament in his office in Corumbá. She was mentally OK, and she knew what she was doing. It is signed by some other people as well."

They stepped into the sunlight. The chief had his arms folded over his chest—he wanted them to leave. Nate removed the camera from his bag and took pictures of the hut and the graves. He made Jevy hold her will while he knelt by her grave.

They found the trail and headed for the woods. As the trees grew thicker, Nate turned for one last look at her hut. He wanted to take it with him, somehow transport it to the States and preserve it. Then the millions of people she helped would have a place to say thanks. But that was the last thing she would want.

The chief said something as they got into their boat.

"He says he doesn't want us to come back," Jevy said.

"Tell him he has nothing to worry about."

The chief was already walking away, toward his village. Nate wondered if he missed Rachel. She'd been there for eleven years. Was he sorry she was gone? Or was he relieved that his gods and spirits now ruled again? What would happen to the Ipicas who were Christians now?

Jevy stopped the motor and guided the boat with a paddle. The current was slow and the water was smooth. Nate carefully opened the satellite phone. Within two minutes, he was talking to Josh.

"Tell me she signed the letter!" Josh shouted.

"You don't have to shout, Josh. I can hear you."

"Sorry. Tell me she signed it."

"She signed a letter, but not ours. She's dead, Josh. She died two weeks ago. Malaria. She left a will, just like her father."

"Do you have it?"

"Yes. It's safe. Everything goes into a trust. I'm the trustee. What happens now?"

"Nothing happens," Josh said. "Troy Phelan's will is paid out. His estate goes to Rachel. It happens all the time in car accidents. The husband dies one day, then the wife dies the next day. The money goes from estate to estate. The settlement has already been agreed. The other heirs will get their money, or what's left of it after the lawyers take their cuts. Read the will to me."

Nate read it, very slowly.

"Hurry home," Josh said.

Jevy had listened to every word of the will. When Nate put the phone away, he asked, "Is the money yours?"

"No. The money goes into a trust."

"What is a trust?"

"It's like a big bank account. Every day it earns more money and I decide where that extra money goes."

♦

They found the boat late in the afternoon. Welly was fishing. Nate called Josh again.

"Call the jet back from Corumbá," he said. "I don't need it. I'm going to take my time coming home. The Phelan lawsuit is settled. There's no rush."

Jevy was at the wheel of the boat. Welly sat below, in the front, his feet just above the water. Nate tried to sleep, but the noise of the engine kept him awake. He watched the river.

Somehow she'd known that he wasn't a drunk anymore, that his addictions were gone. She'd seen something good in him. Somehow she knew he was searching. She'd found a purpose for him. God told her.

Jevy woke him after dark. "We have a moon," he said. They sat in the front of the boat, following the light of the full moon as the river flowed toward the Paraguay.

"The boat is slow," Jevy said. "Two days to Corumbá."

Nate smiled. He didn't care if the journey took a month.

ACTIVITIES

Chapters 1–3

Before you read

1 Look at the Word List at the back of the book. What are the possible connections between these words?

    a *alligator* and *swamp*

    b *will* and *testament*

    c *estate* and *heir*

    d *mosquito* and *malaria*

2 Read the Introduction and answer these questions.

    a What job has Nate O'Riley been given?

    b What is your opinion of Troy Phelan's actions? What kind of person do you think he is? Why?

    c What do you know about the Pantanal?

    d Why is there a lot of opposition to the building of Hidrovia?

3 Discuss, giving reasons:

    a whether you would like to visit the Pantanal region of Brazil

    b whether you think the proposed destruction of wetlands is an important issue

While you read

4 Write the names of the characters.

    a .... is the mother of T.J., Rex, Libbigail, and Mary Ross.

    b .... is Phelan's daughter from his second marriage.

    c Phelan's fourteen-year-old son by his third wife is ....

    d .... has been Phelan's servant for thirty years.

    e .... is Phelan's lawyer.

    f .... has a fortune worth eleven billion dollars.

    g Rachel Lane is the illegitimate daughter of Phelan and ...., who is now dead.

h .... is Rex Phelan's lawyer.

i The government is chasing .... for non-payment of taxes.

j .... is the judge for the Phelan case.

After you read

5 Discuss with other students what you learned about:

  a Phelan's feelings for his three families

  b the signing of the will in the presence of psychiatrists

  c the existence of another will

  d Phelan's final wishes

6 Answer these questions.

  a How much money does Phelan leave his children?

  b What will happen if his children contest the will?

  c Why does he leave nothing to his ex-wives?

  d Where is Rachel Lane and who does she work for?

  e How do Phelan's children feel about his death?

  f How is Rachel's life different from the lives of her half-brothers and sisters?

7 What is your opinion of Nate O'Riley? Do you feel sympathy for him? Why (not)? Will he be capable of finding Rachel, do you think?

Chapters 4–6

Before you read

8 Find out more information about the Pantanal. What will Nate find there? What dangers will he find, do you think? How will he try to find Rachel Lane?

9 Phelan's six legitimate children expect to become very wealthy. When they learn of his last will and testament, what do you think they will do? Why?

While you read

10 Are these sentences true (T) or false (F)?

    a Valdir Ruiz warns Nate of cows on the airstrips,
alligators, and flooding.   .....

    b Milton, Jevy, and Nate survive a plane crash.   .....

    c An army helicopter flies the three men back to
Campo Grande.   .....

    d After Nate drinks five beers, he feels guilty.   .....

    e Rachel's mother sold her to a minister and his wife
for ten thousand dollars.   .....

    f Troy met Rachel when she was a teenager.   .....

    g Nate drinks vodka because he feels very lonely.   .....

11 Write the missing word or name in each sentence.

    a Welly is waiting for Jevy and Nate on the ....

    b Nate puts .... on his arms and legs before he begins
reading Josh's papers.

    c .... promised Rachel never to tell anyone where
she is in South America.

    d Rachel sends and receives mail only in .... and
August.

    e The Phelans' legal teams know that their greedy clients will
agree to .... the will.

After you read

12 Who says this to whom and why?

    a "Their culture hasn't changed for 1,000 years."

    b "This man has four small children and a pretty wife."

    c "Does he take American Express?"

    d "He drowned in a storm."

    e "Did you prepare his last will?"

13 In Chapter 6, what do you learn about

    a Nate's addiction to alcohol?

    b the journalists and lawyers' reactions to Phelan's last will?

    c Rachel's feelings for Troy Phelan?

Chapters 7–9

Before you read

14 Read the titles of Chapters 7–9. What do you think will be the biggest problem for Nate? Why?

15 Discuss what you think will happen to Troy Phelan's money if Rachel refuses to accept it. If she does accept it, how do you think she will use it?

While you read

16 In which order does Nate learn this information? Write the numbers 1–8.

    a Rachel only met her father once.   .....

    b Most Indians had died by the end of the twentieth century, from disease and weapons.   .....

    c Nate and Jevy cannot leave until the chief allows them to go.   .....

    d Hidrovia will link five South American countries but will drain the Pantanal.   .....

    e There is a woman missionary living with the Ipicas.   .....

    f Large companies are letting chemicals flow into the Pantanal.   .....

    g Rachel is both a missionary and a doctor.   .....

    h Rachel does not plan to leave, and money means nothing to her.   .....

17 Which phrase completes each sentence correctly? Circle a or b.

    a Phelan signed the first will in front of the video …

        1) Troy Phelan.

        2) Mickey Mouse.

    b Rachel does not want Phelan's money because she has not earned it and …

        1) she did not know him.

        2) she hated him.

c According to Nate, if Rachel does not accept the money, it will …

    1) be wasted.

    2) be used well.

d Rachel teaches Nate how to …

    1) stop drinking.

    2) pray.

After you read

18 What effect do these have on Nate?

    a He learns about the history of Brazil.

    b The chief informs Jevy that they had taken a wrong turn onto the River Guató.

    c The sky becomes black and the rain suddenly falls harder.

19 How does Snead feel about Troy Phelan's children? Why? How does he offer to help the Phelan family's lawyers? How important is his evidence?

20 Work with another student. Have this conversation.

    Student A: You are Nate O'Riley. You are walking with Rachel toward the funeral in the next village. Try to persuade her to accept the money. Tell her about each of her brothers and sisters. Explain why the money would be dangerous in their hands.

    Student B: You are Rachel. Explain to Nate why you do not want to accept the money. Tell him what you would like him to do about it.

Chapters 10–12

Before you read

21 Will the relationship between Nate and Rachel change, do you think? Why (not)? Will she change her mind about accepting the money?

22 Read the titles of these chapters. Who do you think each one is about? What will happen?

23 Discuss whether you think Hark Gettys will accept Snead's offer. Is Snead as bad as the Phelan children in your opinion? Why (not)?

While you read

24 Tick (✓) the statements that are correct.

    a The local doctor admires Rachel's work.   .....

    b Phelan never gave Rachel money in his lifetime.   .....

    c Rachel wants Nate to tell his partners that he never found her.   .....

    d Nate catches malaria.   .....

    o Rachel visits the boat to take care of him.   .....

    f Gettys signs Snead's contract and gives him half a million dollars.   .....

    g Jevy finds Rachel in Corumbá.   .....

    h Nate confesses his weaknesses to God in a church.   .....

    i Josh persuades Nate to lie to the judge.   .....

    j Nate drinks beer in Josh's house on Chesapeake Bay.   .....

    k Snead will say whatever the lawyers want him to say.   .....

    l Representing Rachel will be Nate's last case.   .....

    m Neva Collier sends Nate's letter to Rachel immediately.   .....

After you read

25 Discuss with another student what you know about the relationships between these people.

    a Rachel and the local tribal doctors

    b Rachel and Nate

    c Snead and Nicolette

    d Father Phil Lancaster and Nate

26 Do you think that Rachel was in the hospital room in Corumbá? Why (not)? Why does Nate think that it is strange that Rachel did not call anyone at World Tribes?

27 Why do you think Nate has decided to give up law? What do you think he will do instead?

Chapters 13–15

Before you read

28 Read the titles of these chapters and discuss these questions.

    a What do you think will happen to Phelan's estate? Will Rachel take the money or will it go to her brothers and sisters?

    b Will Nate return to the Pantanal? What will happen between him and Rachel?

    c Will Nate start drinking again or will he put his life in order?

While you read

29 Who is Nate talking to?

    a "What would have happened if your father had signed the other will and not the handwritten one? And then he jumped? Would he be crazy?" ....

    b "I want to hold my kids and apologize for being such a bad father." ....

    c "And you didn't tell anyone that he was crazy?" ....

    d "Did Mr. Phelan have any marks on his body?" ....

    e "Why did you drop out of school?" ....

    f "I want to see her, but I'm not sure she wants to see me." ....

30 What happens to the money? Write the missing words.

On Rachel's behalf (but without her knowledge), Nate agrees to a settlement of **a)** .... for each heir, which will be shared with their lawyers. This will make Hark Gettys, for example, **b)** .... richer. The rest of the estate, following Rachel's true wishes, will be put into a **c)** .... She appoints **d)** .... to manage the money.

After you read

31 Discuss with other students how Nate feels at the end about:

    a Christi, Angela, and Austin

    b Daniel

    c Kaitlin

    d Rachel

    e Rachel's hut

32 Discuss these questions.

    a In your opinion, was Nate right to act as Rachel's lawyer and settle the lawsuit in the way he did? Why (not)? Does Grisham think that Nate has behaved well?

    b Do you feel sorry for Nate O'Riley at the end of the story? Why (not)?

33 If Troy Phelan could comment on the way the story ended, what do you think he would say?

Writing

34 Write about Nate's problem with alcoholism from his point of view in a letter to his son Daniel. How did it ruin his life and the lives of his two families? How did he finally end his addiction? What is his advice to his son regarding the drinking of alcohol?

35 How did great wealth ruin Troy Phelan's life and the lives of his three families? Could Phelan have used his wealth more wisely? Was he wise to leave it Rachel? Had he learned from his mistakes? Write your opinion.

36 Jevy has learned a lot of strange things about American families and customs from Nate O'Riley. He wants Nate to help him go to the States. Will he like it there do you think? Why (not)? Write your opinion.

37 Write one of Nate's letters to Rachel from St. Michaels, describing the small town and the people who live there.

38 Write an article for a newspaper after Rachel's death, summarizing her life and experiences.

39 Imagine that you are Nate O'Riley. Write a page in your diary after you learn about Rachel's death. Describe the effect Rachel had on your life, and what you thought of her.

40 Contrast the lifestyles and personalities of Rachel and Troy's six other children. Explain how Phelan's money affected them and why.

41 Write a brief description of any two characters in this novel. Consider their actions and why they behave in the way they do.

42 Write a letter to the Phelan heirs and tell them what you think of them. Tell them how you feel about the settlement and the Rachel Trust.

43 What does Nate's sense of humor tell us about him? Using examples from the story, explain how his sense of humor sets him apart from the other characters.

WORD LIST

airstrip (n) a long, narrow piece of land that has been cleared so planes can fly from it

alligator (n) a large reptile with a long body, a long mouth, and sharp teeth that lives in hot, wet areas

charge (v) to put electricity into a piece of electrical equipment like a battery

cremate (v) to burn the body of a dead person

deckhand (n) a member of ship's or boat's crew who does manual labor

dengue (fever) (n) a very serious tropical disease caused by the bite of an infected mosquito

estate (n) all of a person's money and property, especially what is left after someone dies

file (v) to record officially something like a complaint or a legal case

hammock (n) a large piece of material or a net that hangs between two trees or poles and that you can sleep on

heir (n) someone who will legally receive the money and property of a person who has died

illegitimate (adj) born to people who aren't married to each other

lawsuit (n) a problem or complaint that someone brings to a court of law

malaria (n) a disease common in hot countries that is caused by the bite of an infected mosquito

mission (n) an important job that involves traveling somewhere; the work of a **missionary**, a person who goes to a foreign country to teach people about Christianity

mosquito (n) a small flying insect that bites and sucks the blood from people and animals, sometimes spreading diseases

navigate (v) to find the way to a place

paddle (n/v) a short pole with a wide, flat end, used for moving a small boat across water

psychiatrist (n) a doctor who studies and treats mental illness

rash (n) a lot of red spots on someone's skin, caused by illness or by a reaction to something like a plant or food

repellent (n) a substance that keeps insects away from you

satellite (n) a machine that has been sent into space, used for electronic communication

settle (v) to decide on something; to fall to the ground and stay there; to put yourself in a comfortable position; to make an agreement, for example a financial one, that ends an argument; to build a new town or village where no one has lived before

suicide (n) the act of killing yourself

swamp (n) land that is always very wet, and is sometimes covered with water

testament (n) another word for **will**; a statement of belief

tribe (n) a social group of people who live in one area and have the same beliefs, customs, and language

tributary (n) a river or stream that flows into a larger river

trust (n) an arrangement by which someone legally controls your money or property, usually until you reach a particular age

vodka (n) a strong, clear alcoholic drink, first made in Eastern Europe

will (n) also **will and testament**; a legal document in which you say what should happen to your property after you die

The Chamber
John Grisham

The horror of death row is that you die a little each day. The waiting kills you.

Seventy-year-old Sam Cayhall is on Mississippi's death row. Sam hates lawyers but his date with the gas chamber is close, and time is running out. Then Adam Hall, a young lawyer arrives. Can he and his secret persuade Sam to accept his help?

Captain Corelli's Mandolin
Louis de Bernières

Louis de Bernières is one of the best writers in English today.

This is a great love story set in the tragedy of war. It is 1941. The Italian officer, Captain Corelli, falls in love with Pelagia, a young Greek girl. But Pelegia's fiancé is fighting the Italian army ...

Captain Corelli's Mandolin is now a film, starring Nicolas Cage.

Oliver Twist
Charles Dickens

His mother is dead, so little Oliver Twist is brought up in the workhouse. Beaten and starved, he runs away to London, where he joins Fagin's gang of thieves. By chance he also finds good new friends – but can they protect him from people who rob and murder without mercy?

There are hundreds of Penguin Readers to choose from – world classics, film adaptations, modern-day crime and adventure, short stories, biographies, American classics, non-fiction, plays ...

For a complete list of all Penguin Readers titles, please contact your local Pearson Longman office or visit our website.

www.penguinreaders.com

Longman Dictionaries
Express yourself with confidence!

Longman has led the way in ELT dictionaries since 1935. We constantly talk to students and teachers around the world to find out what they need from a learner's dictionary.

Why choose a Longman dictionary?

Easy to understand

Longman invented the Defining Vocabulary – 2000 of the most common words which are used to write the definitions in our dictionaries. So Longman definitions are always clear and easy to understand.

Real, natural English

All Longman dictionaries contain natural examples taken from real-life that help explain the meaning of a word and show you how to use it in context.

Avoid common mistakes

Longman dictionaries are written specially for learners, and we make sure that you get all the help you need to avoid common mistakes. We analyse typical learners' mistakes and include notes on how to avoid them.

Innovative CD-ROMs

Longman are leaders in dictionary CD-ROM innovation. Did you know that a dictionary CD-ROM includes features to help improve your pronunciation, help you practice for exams and improve your writing skills?

For details of all Longman dictionaries, and to choose the one that's right for you, visit our website:

www.longman.com/dictionaries